Hell's Reunion

A Lucas Rook Mystery

To Randy
Cheers!

Richard Sand

Printed in the United States of America.

For information address:
Durban House Publishing Company, Inc.
7502 Greenville Avenue, Suite 500, Dallas, Texas 75231

Library of Congress Cataloging-in-Publication Data
Sand, Richard, 1943 -

Hell's Reunion / Richard Sand

Library of Congress Control Number: 2006935298

p. cm.

ISBN: 1930754965

First Edition

10 9 8 7 6 5 4 3 2 1

Visit our Web site at
http://www.durbanhouse.com

Also by Richard Sand

Fiction

Tunnel Runner
Private Justice
Hands of Vengeance
Watchman with a Hundred Eyes

Non-Fiction

Protocol–The Official Handbook of Diplomatic,
    Governmental and Social Usage

For my old friend, John Warnock

"Where we are is Hell. And where Hell is, there must we ever be."

—Christopher Marlowe

1

Catherine Wren had told Lucas Rook that his need for revenge, his "private justice," was guilt that he was the twin brother still alive. Cholly, the shrink, called it "unresolved duality," whatever that meant, that he felt the World was bad intentions that needed straightening out.

Maybe things would be better if he listened to his on again-off again girlfriend and the shrink. Maybe he should let it go after he had avenged Kirk's murder. Right. And maybe he should grow a pair of tits.

Rook stretched out his bad leg under the seat in front of him and dozed sitting up as only a cop can do. The flight was quick and cheap.

At the car rental, Lucas reached into his pocket for an upgrade. He was flying economy on a bullshit job for a shyster lawyer, but no way he was driving a rice burner compact.

He rolled out in the Buick. The air was clean, the sky blue. Maybe Dustin Hoffman had it right about Florida, "going where the weather meets my clothes."

The ride south on I-75 was straight and quick to the Lakewood Palms Corporate Center. If everything else went as smoothly, he could get an earlier flight back and be in New York for a steak and a beer or two.

Rook swung around the office complex and parked in the back of the tinted glass building. He rode up to the fourth floor and walked down one flight to the developer's office. Rook's bull-shit smile got one back from the receptionist.

"Mr. Fryman will be with you shortly," she said. "There's complimentary orange juice in the carafe."

"I guess that means 'pitcher.'" Lucas picked up a copy of the *Herald Tribune*. A woman wading at Crescent Beach had been bitten by a shark, the second such attack in the Sarasota area in the last week. Bad things come in threes.

"Mr. Fryman will see you now," the receptionist said. She gestured to the door on her left with her French-tipped manicure.

The tall, thin man stood up from behind his curving desk. He wore a linen suit and lime green shirt and tie. Rook could see neither a weapon or muscles on him.

"You do look like you came right out of a Palm Beach magazine, Mr. Fryman," said Lucas. "You surely do."

"Why thank you, Mr. Appel," said the developer. "Please do sit down. The chairs are ergonomically designed. They'll actually exercise your back, they say." He looked at his computer. "My notes say that you're familiar with the Jackson Hewitt relocation and that you're looking for something mixed-use. We have some remarkable opportunities."

Rook shifted his weight to his good leg. "I have an opportunity for you," he said. Lucas took a pen and the stock certificate from his pocket. "You're going to sign this piece of paper."

"Excuse me," said Fryman.

"Now," said Lucas Rook.

The developer reached for the phone, but Rook pulled it away.

"I don't respond to threats, Mr. Appel."

"Good," said Rook. "I don't threaten." He poked the developer in the larynx with his pen.

Fryman gagged, "You're crazy."

"Probably." Lucas came around the desk. "Lovely view. The palm trees blowing in the wind. The asphalt parking lot three stories down. Then again, sign the back of the stock certificate at the 'X,' you get a couple of your fancy lawyers to say 'duress' or whatever, and your signature doesn't mean squat."

Rook offered the pen again, but this time more gently. "But it does mean something to me, Mr. Fryman. So sign it."

The tall man smoothed his two-hundred-dollar tie and did as he was told. "Are we done here?" Fryman said.

"Unless you want to give me the name of your tailor," said Lucas.

"I don't think so."

"Then thank you for your complimentary orange juice. And careful if you go into the water. I hear it's full of sharks."

Rook was back up the interstate and at the Tampa International Airport in an hour. His flight back was as tickey-tack as the one in, but Rook's strategic show of his gold shield to the stewardess got him an aisle seat. It also got him the kind of smile that meant if he was interested, he probably could get his johnson handled.

The only passengers of note were a couple in the back showing more than the fear of flying. Packing your insides with heroin-filled condoms can do that. There were two fat ladies in flowered dresses that made them look like a sofa and three college girls with dark enough tans that their skin was going to look like Randolph Scott before they had their first divorces.

A family in Cincinnati Reds outfits was in the back. In real life, Junior Griffey was playing his seventeenth, eighteenth year. The old man was a player too. Lucas and Kirk were hoisting beers at the precinct bar and watched him hit a slam to beat the Cubs. But that was then. The Boston Red Sox were doing spring training in Sarasota, not the Reds. And nobody had blown Kirk Rook's life away and left him on the sidewalk, bleeding out.

As they landed, Rook got a flash of wedding ring from the stewardess instead of her phone number. As if he hadn't checked that out before or if that meant a shit. He let the drug mules go and took the shuttle bus over to where he had parked his car. Maybe he could swing by Valerie's and get some human contact now that Catherine Wren had asked him to leave again.

"Just a timeout," Catherine had said. "Not like before."

Lucas started to empty his clothes from the drawers she had set aside for him.

"Please don't, Lucas," she told him.

"Catherine, I don't have…"

She touched her fingers to his face. "I have enough for both of us, Lucas. Just give me some time. I still haven't gotten used to finding a gun in the soap dish."

He put his clothes in a duffel bag. "I wasn't done in the bathroom that time. And I'm saying I don't have enough socks and whatever to be leaving them behind."

Catherine Wren sat down on the bed. "I'll buy you some Nordstrom's. All low-cut and French like you hate," she tried. Then she started to cry. "Will you call me when you get back into the City?" she said.

That was over a month ago. They talked on the phone and had dinner once at a new Italian place in Soho, *Il Dulce*, little portions, pictures of Mussolini with funny hats.

"You seeing somebody else?" Rook had asked over his tiny raviolis.

Catherine's face flushed. "I am not."

"Don't get your Irish up, Cat," he said.

"Okay," she told him. After a piece of rum cake that could have been made in an Easy Bake Oven, they walked over to get a cab. When a man in a pin-stripe suit tried to beat them to the taxi, Rook grabbed his arm, but then let him go.

"You had that look again, Lucas," Catherine said. "But I appreciate your restraint."

"And what look is that?" he said.

"That avenging angel look. The private justice look."

They let the next cab pass by.

"You are mistaken, professor," he said. "That was neither my avenging angel look nor my private justice look. And it's not my mad cop look or my 'I'm about to go medieval on your ass' look. It is rather my intuitive, in touch with my inner child, way sensitive, tree-hugging, Hillary-watching, tofu-eating, 'get the fuck out of my lady's cab or I'll break your sorry ass' look."

"That's different," she said.

"Of course it is, my dear," he told her.

Valerie Moon meant a cold beer and a hot fuck. Lucas called her on the way back from the airport.

"I got to work," Valerie told him. "One of the girls is sick and I need the hours."

"You gotta do what you gotta do," Lucas told her.

"I got to cup your balls while I hum show tunes is what I got to do."

"Deal," said Rook. He swung over to the West Side Highway and home.

2

Rook's cell phone rang as he was pulling into Sid Rosen's garage.

"Can you stop by?" Joe Oren asked.

"Everything alright?"

"It's alright. I just wanted to run something by you."

"Sure," Lucas told him.

Rosen put his glasses on his head and put down his copy of *Samsara* as Rook came in. "The devil's second worst invention, the portable phone."

"I won't ask you what the first one is," Rook said.

"I'll tell you when the moment's more dramatic," the garage-man said. His dog barked from his spot in the back.

"Bear, come on," Rosen said. The German shepherd pup sniffed at Rook and then lay down next to Sid's chair.

"I thought of teaching him that slinking trick for whenever you came in, Lucas, like with Jack Palance in *Shane*. Except that it's not seemly to teach a dog to act foolish. It robs them of their truth."

"Truth, huh, Sidney? That's something to contemplate when I'm old and gray." He put the keys to his Mercury up on the board.

"She runs like a dream, just like you said."

"Dreams are…" Sid started, but Rook had already left for Joe Oren's.

Sam came out of Oren's restaurant. Like always, when he left work, he wore a starched white shirt and Panama hat.

"If your T-bone ain't right it's not on me," he said. "But I can guarantee the sides are going to be just fine as I made them up myself."

"You made them, they're fine," said Lucas.

"You know that," said Sam. "Now you enjoy the other half of my peach pie and have yourself a fine evening." The cook moved on to ride the subway uptown to the half Portuguese woman he had been married to for forty years.

Joe toasted Rook with a glass of cold beer as he came in. "This is my second one, which Jeanie says is anti-social."

Lucas sat down and stretched his leg. "I'll catch up to you, Joe."

Oren went over and checked the steaks.

"Sam told me there was a half a peach pie waiting at the end."

"Your detecting skills are flawless, Lucas Rook. We got about one third of a peach pie for dessert since I wrapped my first cold brew around a piece. Cold brew and peach pie. Life's alright at a time like that. Then it grabs you by the short ones," said Joe.

Lucas drank his beer and waited for Joe Oren to tell him what was on his mind. It was after the steak, greens, and garlic mashed potatoes as the pie was heating up.

"You still know the head of security from over at NYU?" Oren asked.

"If it's still Sandy Abrams, I do. The way things are going over there it's just as likely some lesbian from Syria."

"I need you to talk to him." Joe got up to clear the table.

"I'll reach out to Sandy. What are we talking about?"

"You know it's about Jeanie, Lucas. That's obvious as the freckles on my face. Thank God it's not drugs. Her scare last time was enough for that." He brought the dessert over. "You know she is a good girl."

Joe Oren cut the pie in half. "What we need is chocolate ice cream. Christ, I'm going to be making you play twenty questions about this."

"Figured you tell me what you got to tell me, Joe."

"Good. She didn't do nothing. You know how crazy that place is over there, them Olsen twins walking around in all them baggy clothes and what not."

"Bobo."

"The middleweight? I saw him fight Sugar Ray."

Rook took a forkful of pie. "Not Bobo Olsen, the fighter. Helluva middleweight, though. I saw him beat Joey Maxim and Rory Calhoun at the end of his career."

"The cowboy?"

Rook popped another beer. "We're getting way off track here. Rory Calhoun was a light-heavy, not bad. The Rory Calhoun you're talking about was the movie actor, also not bad." He drank some cold beer. "When I said 'Bobo' I meant what they're calling that dumpster fashion look. You know, bohemian and bourgeois equals 'Bobo.'"

"Right, Lucas, right. Anyways, you got them Olsen girls from TV walking around like they're starving to death, and the loonies at the University saying that everybody is imperialistic or totalitarian or whatnot, and there's a dozen groups fighting over them little hills of asphalt in the park, the 'Save the Mounds' and this coalition and that. 'Dogs Run Free,' that's from a Dylan song, the *Post* said."

"And?"

"Right, Lucas. I get all bent when it comes to my Jeanie girl, bullshit or not. So she gets a 'ticket' from the rent-a-cops and then they want to look at her computer about making phony ID."

Rook ate his dessert. "She hear anything from anybody else?"

"Just from the school, but I don't want it going anywhere or on her record."

Lucas reached over and took a forkful off of Joe's plate. "What'd Jeanie say?"

"She said she doesn't do that and anybody can go online and get phonied-up identification for fifty bucks, but that she didn't."

"I'll talk to Sandy. And I'll get back to you tomorrow. Meanwhile, they got her computer?"

"Nope, she told him it was an invasion of her privacy and that she'd met with the University chapter of the ACLU."

"She did?"

"She didn't. I taught her better than that. Lucas, I appreciate your help."

"Appreciate the dinner, Joe. I'll take care of it."

Lucas Rook walked back to the St. Claire. Home as long as it didn't turn condo or whatever. New York was losing its hotels faster than a whore loses her conscience. The Plaza was gone and along with it almost a thousand jobs and more than five hundred rooms. The St. Regis at 55th and 5th was next. The Warwick, the Stanhope. On what he made, if the St. Claire went, he'd be shit out of luck and heading to Copland, New Jersey.

The new deskman was from Eritrea. Polite immigrant with a British accent who you could pay peanuts. What more could an employer look for? His name tag said "Ribai." Perfect since he was a piece of meat to management. He handed Lucas his mail and called him "Sir," but there was something in his eyes that said "Mau-Mau," lock your door at night and don't read *Something of Value* before you go to bed.

The mail was bullshit, an advertisement for modular log cabins, a statement from the bank on the savings account which had $2215 in it , a dues reminder from the Benevolent Association. His answering machine was flashing.

It was crazy Grace singing to him in a country western twang and asking him if she could get on *American Idol*. Beautiful blind Grace Savoy from next door, who could afford to buy her apartment if it went condo. If he was lucky, when he called her back it would be about taking her out on a fashion shoot, which meant some decent money.

Lucas called Sandy Abrams, a good guy who basically got the blue shaft then landed on his feet. Sandy had put in his time at the 17th then worked his way up to Special Operations before somebody at SOD took his legs out from under him. Then it was either back to precinct work, working as a door shaker or moving on. When Sandy heard that NYU was looking for somebody, he keystoned that when he was in the 1-7, he had helped out an assistant dean who was jammed up with an underaged pros. That and the fact that he looked like half a fag and was not married, was just what NYU was looking for.

"How you doing, you surly prick," Abrams said. "Oops, I'm not supposed to be saying that."

"How's it hanging?" Rook said.

"Or that either. What prompts you calling up an old friend?"

No way was the University going to be listening to anything, but on the phone, you always say as little as possible. "It's a little thing I'd like to run by," said Lucas.

"Maybe we can meet over at Mitera's."

"Good," said Lucas. "You can buy me a cup of coffee in an hour." Let him know it's important.

Rook changed into a sports jacket and a turtleneck so he didn't scream cop and grabbed a cab over to the Village. Too bad he didn't have any Che Gueverra-wear or a baseball cap with a marijuana plant on it, but he did stop at the newsstand and bought a copy of the *Voice*.

Sandy was already sitting in a front booth. He looked pale and tired.

"Look like shit, don't I, Rook?" he said.

"I like the academic touch, the goatee."

"I've had the crap kicked out of me, Lucas. Kidney trouble. Which is why I look like my own grandfather. First they're putting a camera up my dick. Then it's my bladder. Then it's a benign cyst on my kidney. No, it's cancer, no, it's not. Fuck 'em. But enough about me. Nice touch with the *Village Voice* under your arm. You could be just any run-of-the-mill neighborhood Trotskyite, Progressive Labor, Pro Muslim, Leftist fuck." Abrams took a pill and drank his water.

The waiter came over. He had buttons in each earlobe.

"Goldseal tea," Sandy said.

"Make it two."

"It'll make you piss like a race horse, Rook. What can I do for you?"

"My niece, Sandy. Jeanie Oren. Your people want to take a look at her computer. Something about fake ID's."

"The administration is very touchy about that. Couple things make them squirrely. That's one of them. Why, I don't know. If you're old enough to turn queer, or turn your ears into some New Zealand tribal thing, protest the war, the weather, whatever, you should be able to have a couple of beers…"

The tea came. Rook asked for sugar, the waiter frowned. "We have several types of honey, buckwheat, clover…"

"Buckwheat's my favorite, chief."

"That's what I'm talking about. You're still so surly." Abrams took another pill and drank his tea.

"That's me, Sandy. So we're talking nothing here?" Rook said.

"The administration being as passive aggressive as they can be. Still upset they're not Columbia."

"And they're not the Viet Cong," Rook said.

"Exactly. I'll take care of this. Now if you'll excuse me for ten minutes or so, I'm going to try and take a leak."

"Take it easy, Sandy."

"I'll take it any way I can get it."

"Viva Fidel," Lucas told him.

"Viva a good piss," Abrams said.

Rook went over to Washington Square. Lots of fences and wire still up. The chess tables. Little dogs trying to find a place to squat. Jamaicans still slinging dope. It used to be cool. Richie Havens, whatever. Nothing righteous about it anyway, anymore. Ratner's was back open. Maybe a real cup of coffee and decent bagel with schmir.

As the light was changing, Jeanie Oren came running across the street. Her hair was platinum blonde. "Hey, wait," said the white boy with dreds trying to keep up with her.

A white SUV came skidding through the intersection. "Jesus Fucking Christ," said the driver, dropping his cigarette that he cupped like an amulet. "You stupid bitch."

Rook walked over to the vehicle.

"What do you want?" the driver said. He was a big man wearing lots of mean. Traffic was backing up.

"An apology," Lucas said. "That's my niece you're talking to."

"Fuck you." Mean reached under his seat.

Rook had the car door open and his back-up piece against the driver's head before he could straighten back up.

"Jesus Christ," the man said.

"Jesus don't have iron against your skull big enough to kill you dead. Small enough so nobody can see it. Put your left hand on your head and bring the right one up so slow I can see the hairs on your knuckles."

"A hammer. I'm a carpenter. Union. I'm from Jersey. And…"

"You got a dirty mouth."

"If you say so," said the carpenter.

"No, if you say so," Rook told him.

He brought his right hand up in slow motion. "I don't …"

"Repeat after me, Jersey. I've got a dirty mouth."

The sector car rolled up. Rook threw him the four-fingered sign that meant everything was okay. The cruiser pulled away.

"Now let's wrap this up, Jersey." Lucas said, "I've…"

"You're kidding me."

The gun said different.

"Okay, I've got a dirty mouth."

Lucas took the keys from the ignition.

"C'mon," the driver said. "I don't have no spares."

Rook stepped into the street. "Don't want you blocking traffic. You know, don't block the box and whatnot gets you hundred dollar ticket." He keyed the SUV bad and then threw the keys back. "Have a nice day," Lucas said.

Jeanie came over with her friend in tow.

"Are you okay?" she asked.

"Okay?" the boy with the dredlocks said. "He's crazy."

"Take a hike," Jeanie told him.

"Excuse me?"

"You heard me. Take a hike. And don't let the swinging door hit you in the keyster."

Jeanie walked over to Lucas.

"Keyster. That's an old-time word," she said. "I heard my dad say it. It's pretty cool."

"Now it'll be cool for you to get your keyster to class," Lucas told her. "And don't worry about that computer problem. Don't worry about anything at all."

3

The address of Rook's office at 166 Fifth Avenue only meant something to people from out of town, even though the super was now wearing a blue blazer instead of his usual sweatshirt.

"You look elegant, Emmanuel, you certainly do. But what is Tony DiMidio going to say?"

"Who's that?" the super asked.

"Lineman for the Chiefs on their '60s Super Bowl team. You were wearing their sweatshirt last week."

Manny adjusted his shirt collar. "I don't follow sports. The shirts come from the silkscreen company moved out. There's going to be more of that."

The building's management had already fixed up the front by putting a new façade which looked like a lot of mirrors. Then out went the manufacturing tenants. No more plastic, jiggling eyes or little doll's arms in the lobby.

The dental lab managed to stay because of the length of their lease and they didn't need a secure elevator. The photographer next door, who made all the bird noises and never went out, negotiated the inevitable increase in rent by suffocating himself in a plastic bag. An architectural firm wanted the photographer's space and

Rook's, so Lucas agreed to move to a back office without a waiting room so the bump in rent was tolerable. His neighbor on the new floor was a printer who made Lucas brochures with his chess piece screened in the background in exchange for skip-tracing some deadbeat customers.

The brochures didn't bring shit, but his previous brilliant work for the Regal and Union Insurance Companies did. They were happy as clams that his job up in Oneonta had turned out so they could invoke the terrorism exception in the policy covering The Bottle House. Well, thank you to Calvin Treaster and the loony fucks in the Brothers of the Half Moon.

The phone rang.

"My name is Everett Warden, Mr. Rook. We're wondering if you'd like to do a little work for us again. You did so indirectly in that matter that Attorney Shipley handled."

Lucas reached in his middle drawer for the black spiral book in which he kept his list of clients.

"I'm listening, Mr. Warden."

"It's a death claim here in New York City. We like to work with local people, particularly people who save us money."

Rook had banged Shipley pretty good for an hourly rate, but he knew he wasn't going to get that from the insurance company.

"I can give you the same rate I billed in Oneonta," he tried.

"I appreciate the gesture, Mr. Rook, but that was the insured paying direct. The best I can do is seventy per hour, and that's only because you're local so the expenses are not an issue."

Rook had already pulled out a package of index cards and started a file.

"Which means what, Mr. Warden?"

"The expenses are yours. Unless they're extraordinary, and then you have to get pre-approval."

"From who?"

"From me, Mr. Rook. I've been handling claims for twenty years anyway, so no, it's not a problem that I'll also be the claims adjuster on the file. I'll be faxing you an engagement letter and a list of guidelines. Please don't deviate, especially in the billing format. Bill monthly, no retainer."

"I bill monthly, you pay monthly, Mr. Warden?"

"Both. We're pretty good about that. The file is 'Helen Maguire.' There's an AD&D rider. Accidental Death and Dismemberment. Costs us another fifty. No murder add-on like we sell the teachers. Here we're looking at the insured's maybe got herself half-lit and falls down the steps because of it. We can show that, there's an exception to coverage. Or if the beneficiary killed her, we pay nothing. Our burden's not like in your criminal case. All we need is the preponderance of the evidence. The claim number will be in the materials, please reference it in all correspondence. Also, don't forget to include a copy of your license, insurance, and bond when you send the signed paperwork back. I look forward to working with you. Incidentally, our insured was divorced. I've already interviewed the ex. So don't, unless you're doing that *pro bono.*"

"Absolutely," said Rook. "No problem." Especially on the *pro bono.* You might just as well be asking me whether I'm going to be Sonny Bono. That's not happening either.

Business clients like insurance companies, banks, whatever, always have a shelf life. They court you or the other way around, you do a good job, you fall in love. Then sooner or later the honeymoon is over. In the meantime, hourly billing, even at that rate, was just fine.

Lucas went over to his shineman. A Jimbo Turner special to herald the new job.

"You're walking good, Mr. Rook. You must be using that peppermint oil I gave you."

"I'm doing good, Jimbo. You got time to give these your deluxe treatment?"

"Well, if Mr. Kissinger and Mr. Johnny Carson show up, they're going to have to wait their time when Lucas Rook asks for the deluxe treatment." He leaned in close to get a good look at the shoes.

"I appreciate that, Mr. Turner. I do."

Jimbo took his first tool from his work apron. "And so does this diabetic, old white shineman." He scored around the edges of the shoes. "Top is good, Mr. Rook. You take care of these shoes. They'll outlast both of us." He took a stick match from his apron and singed off a fraying thread.

Jimbo Turner used a separate rag to wipe on and off the naptha, then a brush of commercial wash. "Timing's just right, like in cooking, Lucas Rook. Me, I'm a bacon and egg man. Always have bacon, four eggs in the morning, four at night, excepting when a friend of mine bring me that Jersey corn or them sweet New Jersey tomatoes. Then I just eat them up with some pepper and salt and I'm richer than a king."

"I'll make it a point," said Rook.

"I know you will," said the shineman.

He dried the shoes and rubbed in a coat of saddle soap with his fingertips, then wiped that down, stopping only when his new hearing aid pinged. Two coats of polish, the first one black, the next one blood before he took his brushes clickety-clack and the two drops of peppermint from the glass bottle so the rag and flannel brought out the mirror shine.

A new customer walked up. "That's not my regular shine," Jimbo told him. "It's with all the extras, if you got the time, and it's twice the price." He gave Rook his shoulder to get down, used his whisk broom, and took the fiver.

"You're more than most of any two men, my friend," Jimbo Turner said. "I thank you for your faith and courtesies." He gave Rook a little bow. "Now don't forget to stop in the Garden State for that produce," Jimbo said to Rook. "I know you won't."

The alarm clock was going off in his stomach, so Lucas went back to Joe Oren's. Let him know that everything was taken care of with Jeanie and get some decent food to take out to Tuze at the Policeman's Home. It would be a good idea anyways to get out there two Tuesdays in a row so they'd be thinking that's when he'd be showing up. Then he comes out there on a Monday next time and catches them they got Ray Tuzio, who was ten times the man they'd ever be, tranked-out and sitting in his own shit.

On the way out to the Home he'd stop at a CVS and get some Camay soap for the LPN's, "Loser Prick Nothings," to steal and some Ensure and Depends. Jesus Christ, the guy who taught him the streets and saved his life, particularly that time he come in with his riot gun, is wearing diapers. Diapers and his aviator sunglasses, which if they got lifted, there always had to be another pair to replace them.

Joe and Sam and Jeanie, her wearing her gambling hat, were in the back of the restaurant playing rummy.

Joe looked at his watch, then shook his wrist. "Must be broken or something, huh, Jeanie?"

"My class was canceled, Daddy."

"Well your poker face be telling me it ain't," said Sam.

"I'm refining my skills here, people. Everybody at school thinks they're expert from playing poker on the computer. They're no match for the Manhattan Kid, though." She took off her pork-pie and turned it over. "You ever play hat? You try and sail them into…"

"Before you were born, missy. You got class?" asked Lucas.

"We're done for the day."

"Then do your homework or do the dishes."

"And my grease trap needs cleaning," Sam said.

"I think I can find a study group. For serious." Jeanie Oren went around the table kissing them each on the cheek. When she got to the door she came back and gave her dad another one.

"That's my girl," Joe Oren said when she left. "Got to watch her with these fads of hers, though. Rock climbing, train spotting, her senior year in high school it was spelunking, whatever that was."

Sam shuffled the deck like he meant business.

Joe got up to get some hot coffee. "Tell Sandy I owe him, Lucas."

"Him and not the University forever charging Fifth Avenue prices to teach the kids to be revolutionary and fashion plates or whatever." Rook turned over his hole card.

Sam showed his ace of hearts. "Pay the dealer," he said. "The Manhattan Kid ain't the onliest one can play these skins."

Oren poured out the hot coffee.

"Going out to see Tuze," Rook said.

"He doing alright?"

"He's alright, Joe."

"I'll make him some mac and cheese," said Sam.

Rook read the claims material sent over by Everett Warden. Helen Maguire was fifty-two years old when she fell down the basement stairs of her building or got beaten to death, depending on which version you were buying. Divorced six years ago. Her son was killed in Iraq. The secondary beneficiary was Helen's brother with the Hell's Kitchen address. NYPD had come up with nothing, or at least nobody had taken a pinch yet.

One of the claims notes referenced an inquiry to the insurance company from a Detective D. Graves regarding the beneficiary of the life insurance. Lucas wondered if it was Hy Gromek's partner. Hy was a good guy. Dwight Graves was a pain in the ass. Then again, Hy Gromek was dead and his partner wasn't, which maybe says something about the world.

Rook called over to the precinct to chat Graves up. Find out who the riding ADA was and maybe get some decent info. Certainly get some billing out of it.

The call got it was the same Detective Graves who had partnered up with Hy, but his shift was over and tomorrow was his RDO. A couple of laughs with the desk got Lucas the name of the assistant district attorney, whose name was Collins. Some we're on the same team, rah-rah got Rook a meeting with the ADA. The case and the meter were starting to run just fine.

4

Assistant District Attorney Michael William Collins lit his dying cigarette with another.

"You alright?" Rook asked him.

"I'm good," the ADA answered through an exhale of smoke. "People think I chain-smoke, I got a problem. Fact is I love the nicotine."

"I can see that. You got time for a beer?"

Collins looked at his watch. "That I do, but I don't drink. One vice is good enough if you love it the way I do." He took two quick drags and then a deeper one. "I'd rather just walk and smoke if you don't mind."

You're talking outside, you're giving away information even if you're walking, but it was Michael who was going to do the talking. "That's okay with me," Lucas said. "We can grab a Sabrettes unless you don't eat meat."

Collins finished his smoke and popped a Halls. "If you call a hot dog meat, I do." He lit another cigarette and inhaled the smoke over the menthol lozenge.

"You said you were working for an insurance company, Mr. Rook. I'm not supposed to be discussing any cases, open or closed, even if you were on the job for all those years." He took another deep drag. "But frankly, I'm halfway out the door and my section chief is a hard on anyway."

"Looking at the private sector, Attorney Collins? Trying cases the way you do, you've got the perfect resume for a defense firm or in-house for an insurance carrier looking for somebody with the killer instinct."

An old woman holding an ice pack on her jaw pushed between them.

"Hell hath no fury like a woman coming from the dentist," said Collins.

"Unless it's the dentist," said Rook.

The lawyer dropped his cigarette and rubbed out the butt with his tasseled loafer. He reached for another smoke, then stopped. "I'm very considerate about not disturbing others' dining experience," Collins said.

There was a line at the hot dog stand. Some men in suits and two in Con Ed uniforms. A cabbie pulled over to the curb.

"Wait your turn," a repairman said.

"He's a regular," said the vendor.

"He should go to the end of the line," said one of the suits.

"My order's ready, gents," said the taxi driver. "Two loaded. Three grape sodas."

It was Bobby Haak. He recognized Lucas Rook and that he might need a friend.

"Detective," he said. "How ya doin'?"

"Just trying to get my chow like the rest of the folks in line."

"I hear you. You guys get a pretzel on me," said Bobby and he swung away.

Rook and Collins ate as they walked across the street. The prosecutor started over to a group of office workers that were smoking.

"We're talking about the Helen Maguire case," Lucas said.

"Right, it's the call of the nicotine." He lit up again as they went up the block, his hot dog in one hand, his smoke in the other. "Right, I was the riding DA. Knowing what to do with a case is as much as trying it. Helen Maguire was a white female. Good looking for her age, but on the beefy side. Great red hair, but judging from the fact that she was a beautician, it probably wasn't real. I meant to ask if her collar matched her cuffs, but didn't get around to it."

"How do you read it? The steps do her in or somebody break her head?" Rook asked.

"Couldn't tell from the injuries, really. There was a lot of blood, but the splatter pattern was inconclusive. Not like on television or whatever." He looked at his watch. "Got to get back to the office. My boss is a prick. Anyway, there was no robbery and no sexual assault. I know you're looking at the insurance angle, but my guess is she just fell. Her blood alcohol was below limit."

"Any family?" Lucas asked.

"Divorced years ago. The ex is living in Vermont. Her kid got blown up in the war, which nobody should be there in any case."

He checked his watch again. "Then again, it may run in Helen's family. She has a brother lives in Hell's Kitchen who is a stone alcoholic."

They were in front of the district attorney's office.

"You developed some fine case material here, counselor," said Lucas.

"Credit goes to the lead detective, Dwight Graves. Looks just like Bill Cosby." He flicked his cigarette into the street. "I kept expecting him to say something about Jell-O. No way the Cos molested those women with all the money he's pulling down. All he has to do is make a phone call and a Halle Berry look-alike is there." He reached for another cigarette and then put it back. "I try the case though, Cosby, he's as good as sentenced."

Michael William Collins took a can of dip out of his jacket pocket and put a pinch of smokeless tobacco between his cheek and gum. "I know it would help you if you got to see my file, but I got ethics. Just because I'm a nicotine fiend…"

Rook handed over one of his business cards with the chess piece on it. "Send me your resume. I'll see what I can do."

"Appreciate it," said Collins. He took one of his own cards and gave it to Lucas. "I know how to handle a case," he said.

"The insurance company will appreciate what you said and so forth. I know they will," Rook said. He used the ADA's card to clean the hot dog gristle from his teeth as he walked away.

Lucas stopped at the drug store for some Tums. It was easier when he was on the Nexium, which he got out of date from Wingy Rosenzweig for pennies. He could eat onions, garlic, whatever, but the doc took him off the "little purple pill" for whatever reason. Tums and some aftershave and those little sticks you clean your teeth and gums with. Some genius made a fortune who figured that one out. A zillion percent profit.

The cashier at the drugstore looked familiar. Face a lot fuller, but still those blue-green eyes looking like opals or whatever, with her black skin and the half-smile on her face meaning she knew something you didn't.

"Well, how you doing, Mr. Rook?"

"How you doing, Darlene?"

"I'm pretty as ever except from waiting for you to call."

"I'll stop back to see you," he said as he handed over his ten.

"I'm in a hurry," said the woman next in line.

"Register three will take you, Mrs. Rosenthal, and your feminine products. I'm here talking to my financial consultant."

The lady moved away.

"Financial consultant, Darlene?"

"Could be," she said.

"You take care," Lucas said.

"Take it slow and smooth," she said.

Rook went back to the office. Somehow it wasn't the same without the unused waiting room and the crazy photographer next door making sounds like the bird house at the zoo. Manny looked resplendent in his non-sweat shirt.

"Good afternoon, Emmanuel. You look elegant."

"Right," Manny told him. "I'm going to go unstop the toilet on the third floor for the second time this week already. That asshole in the dental supply puts paper towels in the bowl."

"I'll be scrupulous to avoid same, Emmanuel," Lucas said.

Rook had enough to start his billing. You don't charge for the first conversation with the claims adjuster or reviewing their policies and procedures. But you get the time in elsewhere, memos to file and whatnot. As it looked now, he'd have the meeting with Dwight Graves and had the son KIA in Iraq and the Hell's Kitchen brother to look at. And maybe with some decent spadework he'd find some other angles.

The phone rang. It's Christmas with strippers under the tree you get two new clients in the same week.

"It's me," Grace Savoy said in a bad Russian accent.

"Let me guess," Lucas said. "Stalin, Kruschev, Molotov."

"They're cocktails, right, Lucas Rook? You asking your hot blind neighbor supermodel out for a drink?"

Rook moved the papers around on his desk so he could see his desk calendar. "You called me, Gracey."

"So I did. I guess you can guess they're doing a re-shoot of my vodka ad tonight. Lawrence thinks it's too too."

"Too what?"

"Too something or other. I told him it's time and a half. For both of us. Can you come? Please, please. Midnight at the Goethals Bridge. I'm wearing a white mink."

He started putting his paper in a pile. "I've got an appointment tomorrow morning."

"Grace Savoy dyed her landing strip to match her coat, Lucas."

"That's more than I need to know. How long is the job going to take?"

She opened a beer. "Two, three hours."

"Messes up my dance card, Gracey."

"Kenny died, Lucas Rook. My driver, my friend. He just died. His heart exploded."

"I'd worry if I had one, Gracey."

"Then you'll come?"

"I'll have my car downstairs," Lucas said, "but I'm not listening to Lawrence or whoever, and only if you're paying me."

"Deal," she said. "They're sending a car. I'll ring your bell at eleven," Grace said. "So we'll have enough time for you to see my…"

"Work," he told her. "And I'll get you."

"I should be so lucky," said Gracey in a bad Russian accent.

5

The nicotine-fiend ADA's talking about the medical examiner's findings, any investigator worth anything's going to take it the next step, especially when the ME's office was just across town at 23rd and First.

"Open 24-7," OCME proudly announced and the office was open around the clock. The assistants to the chief, Charlie Hirsch, were first rate, and so were the techs and the docs, not like that dwarf asshole from Philly who was on the Heather Raimondo case.

Lucas went over with a clean notebook in his inside pocket. With a little luck he'd come back with a half-dozen of the narrow pages filled front and back, which not only would give him the info he needed, but some decent billing from the interview and the write-up.

Woody was still at Intake, working on another degree.

"What is it this time, Woodman?" Rook asked.

Haywood looked up from his text. "Cost analysis of something or other, Rook. What brings you to this party store?"

"The usual."

Woody handed him over a visitor's badge. "Glad you didn't say 'Truth.' I hear a lot of that. Death-Truth. Which I guess is why I'm in school my whole life, trying to figure out how they, whatever."

"You do, send me a card, Woody. You got your nose in your books, or taking a leak on my way out, I'll leave your badge in the tub."

Lucas Rook went down the hall and then through the office like he belonged in the place. Path, toxicology, the lab.

"You must be lost," called a voice from behind him.

It was Carolyn. He hadn't seen her much in the last few years, but some people you form something with, it's like you just were sharing a pitcher the night before. Especially when they've been through the stuff you'd rather forget.

"Dr. Marker," Lucas said. "I'm waiting to buy you a cup of coffee."

"The cof in the caf awaits," she said.

They went down to the cafeteria. Carolyn had a piece of whole wheat bread with her coffee. Lucas had a bad piece of pound cake.

"You back from New Orleans to stay?" Rook asked her.

"Nothing 'easy' about 'the Big Easy.' But I figured I got all but about ten thousand pieces left over from the WTC, I had to go somewhere and relax."

She sipped her coffee. "But you're not here to talk about Katrina or 9-11. And probably not to buy me a cup of coffee either."

"Not that, doc. DOA was Helen Maguire. An insurance job."

"Don't know it. I was probably in New Orleans tagging floaters and writing 'Drowning' a zillion times. Let's go back to my office. I'll get you the file."

Her secretary, a good-looking woman in her 40's with the tits of a teenager, handed her a stack of phone messages.

"Busy, busy," said Carolyn. "Get me Helen Maguire's file, please. And hold my calls."

Rook and Dr. Marker went into her office. There were files on one of the visitor's chairs, a travel bag on the other.

"Coming or going, Doc?"

"I figure that out, will save me a bunch, Lucas."

Her phone buzzed. "They're pulling the file now. We looking for the proximate or the mechanism or both?"

Good deal she wasn't making small talk. No way that wouldn't take them to how she did him the solid by passing on Kirk's autopsy, which was mandated by state statute.

"Most times we have an insurance claim, Lucas, a verbal from the pathologist is sufficient. We have anything sexy here, detective?"

"Other than yourself, Doc, I don't think so. Lady falls down the steps. There's some policy issues."

The pathologist's phone rang again. "Sure, sure, bring it in."

Rook tried not to stare at the secretary's tits on her way in and out from delivering the file. Dr. Marker went through the paperwork. "You're looking for her being wasted as the cause of the fall, Lucas, I'm afraid I'm not going to be too much help. Helen's blood alcohol was .037, less than half the legal. Not to say she wasn't tipping back a few, but your DOA was a big lady, 171 pounds."

"Lot of weight going down the stairs too, Carolyn."

Dr. Marker handed Lucas the file.

"Knock yourself out," she said. "I got to go pee."

Rook knew the language from the job. You had to have the ME take a look when the death was "from criminal violence, by casualty, by suicide, suddenly when in apparent good health, or unattended by a physician or in any suspicious or unusual manner."

He looked through the file for what fit in those slots. "Lethality initiated by fall." And nothing else that mattered.

Carolyn Marker came back in. "You good, Lucas?"

"Good to go, Doc."

They shook hands.

"Take that vacation," Rook said.

"Thinking about it, Lucas. I'm doing that."

Rook went out into the hall and then came back in. She was just picking up the phone to start her return calls, but put it down.

"Forget something, Lucas?"

"To thank you again, Carolyn. For..."

"That's what I do," said Dr. Marker. "Find the answers, provide the endings. When I'm lucky, one means the other. With your brother, it didn't."

Lucas Rook walked a few blocks before waving down a cab. His bad leg was acting up, which should have been no surprise since he needed another operation which he wasn't going to have and he'd stopped doing his exercises. Back at the St. Claire, he poured a cold one and checked his mail and messages. All bullshit, but the money from Grace Savoy would be a good thing until the insurance company started paying on the Maguire job.

He traded his pancake holster for a shoulder rig since he was going out to see Tuze. The jitbags at the Police Home needed a peek at his iron to be reminded they were dealing with cops. Then he walked over to the garage to get Kirk's Avanti.

Sid Rosen was under the hood of a Lincoln LS. "Think they'd change the way the car looks every decade or so, but they don't," said the garageman. "I guess they figure they're better off making the computer so a NASA scientist can't figure it out before the car ain't no good anymore. Planned obsolescence, they call it."

"Going to go out to see Tuze. You want anything from around the corner?"

"Need a couple of cans for the pup here, but only if they got chicken. I know he's not the same as his namesake, but I don't want this pup here coming down with the ear yeast from eating beef. And some chocolate and vanilla ice cream for yours truly. Good old fashioned chocolate and vanilla. No 'Ebony Shards and Alabaster Dreams' or whatever."

The German shepherd came over and lay down in a circle beside the Lincoln.

"And no Ben and Jerry's neither," said the Rosen. "Mumia should rot in jail, the copkiller. And then he can fry in hell."

"There'll be some folks waiting for him there, Sid. I'll be taking Kirk's car out."

"That real estate tycoon, Carrarei, asked about the Avanti again, Lucas."

"Not interested."

Rook knew it was half-stupid to be holding on to his twin brother's car and that he should let it go. But he was no good at that.

He dropped off the dog food and the ice cream for Sid and rode the black fiberglass coupe out to the Policeman's Home with the soap, Ensure, and diapers. They had moved Tuze again, which didn't mean anything to him since he only half knew where he was half of the time. To Lucas Rook it meant plenty. Ray Tuzio, who had been the first one through the door. Raymond A. Tuzio, who had saved his life in Etillio's garage with his riot gun, now sat in his own waste, spent his days and nights looking out that window.

"Can I help you?" asked the gap-toothed woman at the front desk.

"I'm here like I am every week." Lucas walked away and up the hall on the left. A black man in his pajamas shuffled by holding on to the handrail. "Got to roll," he said. "Got to roll."

Tuze was in bed and didn't look up. Neither did the other cop in his room, who spent all his time pulling on his prick.

"How ya doin', partner?" Lucas asked.

"I got to go to the can," said Tuze.

Rook helped him up and took him to the bathroom. There were baby wipes and Depends on the top of the toilet. A big sign, "Do not flush inappropriate objects." Like maybe the half-assed help.

Ray Tuzio had already shit himself. Rook sat him down and called for the pretend nurse to come change him. Bad for her, which she deserved, maybe halfway good for Tuze to have a woman around.

"We attend to continence matters every three hours," said the LPN, who smelled of vodka. Real drinkers think it doesn't leave an odor.

"I'm not talking about North America, South America, whatever, or your time schedule, Ms. Smirnoff, or is it Stoli? Now you attend to my friend here before he gets a rash and I get myself motivated to talk up how you're saucing when you should be nursing."

She adjusted the badge on her blouse. "I will not be bullied," she said.

"Yes you will. Just do your job and everybody's happy."

Ray tried to stand up, but wobbled.

"We should not agitate Mr. Tuzio, now should we?" she said. "Now, let's get you cleaned up and back to bed, Raymond. It's almost time for your meds."

Right. Tranq him good so he doesn't know where he is at all. Rook stopped at the Wings to Fly three blocks away and got himself a six pack of Coors for the way back. Three beers was his limit if he was driving, two if he was working. He wondered if after seeing his old partner like he had, the three brews would do it.

Rook went to Hell's Kitchen to see Helen Maguire's brother to get his mind off of Tuze and get some more billing in. Reds Maguire had himself a pedigree back from when the Irish mob meant something, which was before Mickey Featherstone went rat in '88. Lucas was in the courtroom with the Manhattan Task Force South when Mickey got his walk, the judge telling him the Witness Protection Program was his reward for "a violent past, a redemptive present, and an uncertain future." That could be a lot of people, not just the murdering, psycho drug fiend stoolie Featherstone, who had sold the Westies out. The papers said, "Westies con sings Irish Lullaby."

Reds had done a bit for armed robbery and had a half dozen convictions for assault, two of them on cops and twice that many in the neighborhood commerce of numbers running and working the collecting route for the boys up the line. More than likely Maguire was not going to be a physical threat because of his age and that he'd be in the bag. But no way you could turn your back on him.

Red's cousin, Eddie Kelly, who roomed with him, was a different story. A big, bad dude who had worked for Local 824 when it was called the Pistol Local. Kelly had taken a ball peen hammer and more to dozens and used to help Westie mob boss, Jimmy Coogan, cut up their dearly departed adversaries for neat disposal in black, plastic parcels.

"Clinton" they were calling the neighborhood now, but for anybody who had half a memory or any heart, it was still Hell's Kitchen. The story was a hundred years old: One Irish cop says to the other, "This place is hell itself." The other one gives it back that, "Hell's a mild climate. This is Hell's Kitchen, no less." Now it was the developers and the politicians doing each other for the leavings after the Olympics went in the toilet where they belonged.

When the Westies ran the neighborhood, 11th was called "Death Avenue." The Sunbrite was up and 596 Club, and the White House Bar meant something. Now there was a Volvo dealership and a Starbucks in the neighborhood. Rook parked down the street and walked up to 414 West 49th Street. They were power-washing the front of the brick building, and two queers rushed to get their potted plants off the fire escape.

"You need any help, girls?" said Reds Maguire as he leaned back against the fence of Clinton Gardens.

"Right," said Eddie. "You need any help?"

"Not from you," one of them called from across the street.

"You wish," said Reds.

"You wish," repeated Kelly.

Rook walked up. Time and oceans of alcohol had not been kind to Helen Maguire's brother. Except for his red hair he looked like he was on the bad side of Social Security, but the roomie looked like he could still deal it out and take it too.

Lucas stood outside of Eddie's reach. "Thought you two'd be celebrities like those Noonans in the *New York Times* and what not," Rook said.

"Them two's alright," said Maguire. "But this is chickenshit. Just because of who you are, I'm supposed to talk to you?"

Lucas unzipped his jacket part way. "I run you in a couple of times, Reds?"

"I don't talk to cops about nothing," Kelly said.

"I'm working for your sister's insurance company, Reds," Lucas told Reds.

"About what?"

Rook took a half a step in. "About a whole lot of money. Fifty very large, as you may know. Let's walk around the corner. I buy you a cup of coffee. We can talk."

"You're a cop, as far as I'm concerned," said Maguire. "You got something to show me otherwise?"

"You got some ID?" asked Kelly.

Rook handed them each a business card with the chess piece on it. Reds fired up a Pall Mall. "I'm supposed to kiss your ass or something? This don't mean nothing."

"Means maybe the fifty grand might be flying out the window." Lucas started to walk away. "Give me a call when you're not too busy for the fifty," Rook said. "That SSI don't go like it used to, especially when smokes are five bucks."

Reds came over. "I ain't giving you lip or nothing, and no-body's playing me. But I want what's coming to me."

"You want that cup of coffee or you can…"

"I'll call you later on."

"Right," said Rook. "You do that. Meanwhile, I'll remind my-self just where you remember me from."

You lock somebody up or tune somebody up, you remember who they are. Maybe Reds Maguire had him confused with Kirk, or just as likely he had a thousand or two too many shots and a beer for breakfast.

Rook dropped his car off at Rosen's garage and went back to his apartment to write up his visit with Helen's brother. The job could probably support an hour or so of research as to where Reds knew him from. He'd cogitate on that over the leftover ravioli and meatballs from Maggio's and another beer or two before getting ready for Gracey's job by stretching out on the sofa.

The Yanks would be on soon, still trying to buy their way back to what they had when the ballplayers gave a damn. Lucas checked his office messages. The first was Grace Savoy telling him that Lawrence was a runny little shit and the shoot was cancelled again.

There also was a return call from Dwight Graves using his mean cop voice. "This is Detective Graves. Come on in if you've got something to say."

And a message from the insurance company. "Everett Warden. I'm sending over a fax. Call when you receive it."

The pasta and sofa would have to wait. Lucas Rook went back to 166 Fifth Avenue.

6

The fax was waiting. Helen Maguire's son, Private Henry Maguire, had an interesting business relationship established before an RPG took his head off. That relationship was with Marshall Funding, who was seen regularly on television exhorting the expectant to cash in their birthrights for pennies. Seems they'd bought out Private Henry Maguire's expectation of inheriting from his mother for less than next to nothing.

The bad thing for the insurance company is now they got Marshall Funding at the trough and they're not going to be pushed around. The good thing for Lucas Rook is the fax about Marshall Funding meant heavy billing. Rook spent some time on the computer and made a couple of calls before he got back to Everett Warden.

"I got your fax," Lucas said. "Marshall Funding appears to be a stand-alone. Probably a group of the old add-on lending crowd, bar financing and the like. And no doubt the shysters."

"Essentially correct, Mr. Rook. Actually it was a bunch of PI lawyers. It made perfect sense for them to put together the company. Half of them having to advance money to their clients, anyway. Regardless of what the lawyers' disciplinary rules say."

"Right, to keep the cases they bought to begin with. By the way, Mr. Warden, I don't do accident work."

"We know that, Mr. Rook. We wouldn't have hired you if you did. Your contact at Marshall Funding is Samuel Gordon."

"I'll get out there tomorrow. Is he a liar? I mean lawyer?" An old insurance company joke.

"Used to be, Mr. Rook. Now he can't afford it. I'd like you to get what you can and worry him a bit."

Rook put some notes on an index card. "I can do that."

"No side trips, please. You're getting some expenses here because there's travel, but mileage is one of the things our home office looks at hard. That and T and E."

"I stay away from strip clubs, Everett."

"Not just those, Mr. Rook. Restaurants and so on."

"I was making a bad joke, T and A. Tits and ass, strip clubs."

"Let's set aside the vulgarity, can we," said Warden.

"Right," said Lucas Rook. "No T and A jokes whatsoever."

"I appreciate that, Mr. Rook. And do watch that mileage."

Watch the mileage? It's only sixty miles to Bridgeport. Lucas called over to the garage to tell Rosen he was going to take the Mercury out.

"I'm not here, you take the keys off the board," Sid said. "I'll leave her up front. She runs like a dream like I told you, right, Lucas boy?"

"She does," Rook said. My dream's still running like a freak show, he thought. Last night he had his regular Kirk-is-alive,-but-it's-awfully-cold-and-he's-not-talking-right dream. The twin cop brothers, him and Kirk, they're looking out the window and in it at the same time, whatever that means, and Jimmy Salerno and Chick, who are both dead, are pouring shots and everybody keeps drinking and pouring and yammering. Kirk is bleeding while he talks and all the time everybody is pouring and laughing while his brother is bleeding. Right, she runs like a dream, as if that's a good thing.

Lucas Rook put his .38 snubby under the seat because Connecticut had some wacky gun laws. Like the one from '99 that they could confiscate if they thought you were going to be a danger to yourself or others, which one way or another was him every day. But no way you go anywhere without a piece, not to mention Bridgeport, which got a third Hispanics.

Lovely city, Bridgeport. "Developing the Port," holding on to factory jobs pretty well and only halfway turning into a liberal freak show, mostly because Tony Armeno didn't put on a prick suit when he became chief of the Bridgeport PD.

Last time Lucas worked in Bridgeport nobody busted his balls. He had come up from New York to do some work for somebody who was on his way from mayor to con. Rook didn't usually do defense work, but the mayor was basically a good guy caught in a mess that used to be the way you did business.

Maybe it was because Bridgeport thinks it's glamorous to be a PI, it's the home of Robert Mitchum, who played Philip Marlowe, and Belzer, who couldn't carry his jock, but was still on the tube as Detective Munch, or whatever, but they let Rook do his job last time, so this trip out to squeeze Gordon's shoes looked not to have add-on agro from the authorities.

There was a back-up at Exit 27 to Bridgeport, an overturned Toyota on Lafayette Boulevard, the FD and two EMT vehicles. Not a pretty sight. Or the obese black woman masquerading as a cop while she talked on her cell. Somewhere Gerry DiJoseph was turning over in his grave. It was 1980 when he was shot to death in Bridgeport on a routine car stop. It was the day after Lucas and Kirk had been in the photo "Double Trouble for the Bad Guys." Some brainiac thought it would be good PR if they went up to the funeral together. There was nothing good about it.

It was an off hour at the Coffee Central at 2500 Main Street in Bridgeport, but the coffee was still fresh. So was the counter girl.

"The booth is for two or more," she said.

Lucas picked up the menu. "The joint is empty, dear."

She turned her back. "You could go up the street to Dunkin'

Donuts for all I care."

The owner came out from the back. He had the two-shift, seven-day-a-week look. "Bernadette, pour this man a cup of coffee. Maybe he'll have a piece of pie or whatever."

Lucas picked up the menu. "Pot roast sandwich." Place serves pot roast, they're making their own stuff.

The man slow-moved back to the kitchen. "And a side of mashed, no gravy, Bernadette," Rook told her. He picked up a part of the *Connecticut Post* from the next booth. A swindler crashes his plane after bilking a fortune from some old housewives. A suitable ending, but only if he isn't killed instantly.

The owner came back out. "Name's Smilk," he said. "Like the cow juice, but with an S. Bernadette, she thought she was going to be a princess, marry this doctor type from over at the University for which she gets knocked up, but then he drops her." He put the platter down. "But then again, it's my gain. How else I'm ever going to get close to a young thing like that?" He wiped away an imaginary spot on the table.

The sandwich was good. Perfect cut of meat for a small place. A poor man's meal, you buy it cheap and tough and cook the shit out of it so it's like filet mignon. Like osso buco. He was once doing some private security at a dinner party at a casino in AC. Big black guy, used to be in Washington, is telling how they used to eat "shinebone" after it was in the pot for a day or three.

Bernadette sat at the counter smoking a cigarette, so Rook left his money on the table. When he was gone she'd probably pocket it all. Smilk must know that, but then again probably didn't care as long as she let him rub up against her when the joint was closed.

Marshall Funding was in the 3200 block of Main Street and shared space and probably a bank account with Courtesy Real Estate Sales and the Jensen Law Center. Sammy Gordon was the kind of guy you wanted to slap the first time you met him. Weasely-looking guy with designer glasses.

"Mr. Rook, I was expecting you." His hand was moist. "You're here to discuss the buy-out of an expectancy. Annuities, structured settlements, inheritances, we do them all. We offer excellent and expeditious pay-outs." He walked back and forth behind his desk as he talked.

Rook flashed his old NYPD shield and gave him his tough cop look. "I'm sure you do," he said.

Sammy sat down. "I don't understand."

"Of course you do."

Scare the crap out of him, so he doesn't know what's going on.

"Henry Maguire. Private Henry Maguire. You paid him less than two cents on the dollar."

"Perfectly legal," Gordon said. He sat back down and went into his computer.

Lucas leaned forward. "So you're a lawyer now?"

"Actually I am."

"I bet you own the Jensen Law Clinic and probably the real estate."

"Perfectly legal. Everything is. My file says he signed all the paperwork."

"And now you want a 50-1 return. I don't think so."

Sammy Gordon took out a yellow pad. "Actually, my principals do. And after I see your identification, I'd like to know what you're doing here."

"Union Insurance Company. I'm doing the 'due diligence' routine. Pay a visit, check the paperwork. Ask a few questions. Be the hard-head mean prick I am, if I have to."

Sammy Gordon looked relieved. "Everything's in order. A copy of the Assignment of Proceeds has been sent to Union, so I can show you a copy of that, but the rest is confidential. I do assure you everything's perfectly in order."

Bringing back the whole file would confirm how fortunate Warden and his insurance companies were to have Lucas Rook working for them, even on the monthly retainer they hadn't yet thought of. Lucas leaned forward. "Not if Mr. Maguire made a binding will before he signed with you."

Gordon finger-combed some strands of his hair back to their strategic position. "He took an affidavit that he had not executed any other assignments, transfers or the like and revoked in writing all previous documents, including wills."

"Doesn't matter, Mr. Gordon, I think it's called a 'noncupature will.' That's oral. And it's binding in New York since he was in Iraq at the time. I think that's covered by the phrase 'during a war, declared or undeclared.' The armed forces has a pretty decent procedure of ratifying such wills."

Gordon stood up. "I am an attorney, Mr. Rook, so you needn't lecture me. What proof do you have?"

"As we say in the insurance business, Mr. Gordon, we can do this the hard way or the easy way."

"Meaning what?"

"We litigate the shit out of this, declaratory action in federal court, all of that expensive, time-consuming stuff, or we act like gentlemen. I get to make a living either way. Worse comes to worst, we save Union a sliver of their policy, everybody goes home happy." Rook took an envelope out of his jacket pocket and then put it back. "You show me yours, I show you mine."

"Maybe I can live with that," said Gordon. "My secretary's at lunch." He went into the next room. Rook could hear the copier running. When the lawyer came back he smelled like cigarette. He handed Lucas a copy of six more pages. "And what do you have for me, Mr. Rook?" he said.

"Excuse me?"

"Your confirmation of the oral will?"

Lucas put the papers Gordon had given him into his pocket and gestured with his envelope. "You're welcome to this, Mr. Gordon, but I doubt it will do..."

"Let me be the judge of that, Mr. Rook."

Rook got up. "Fine, counselor. I'm sure with your law degree and all, you'll find my dry cleaning receipts to be of use somehow. Now you have a nice day."

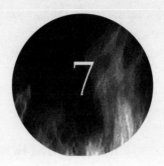

7

Rook waited until he was back in his office before he placed his call to Everett Warden, who was out, probably trying to get some poor injured slob to sign a release for $500 in his hospital room. Lucas faxed over the file material he had gotten from Sammy boy.

Then he took out a pad, not a yellow one, lawyers used them, and roughed out his billing, which he would later enter into Time-slips. The call, the papers he'd gotten from Marshall Funding. Charge .2 for the fax, .9 for review of the papers and .5 for a memo to the file regarding his meeting. Since his billing instructions didn't specifically prohibit the travel time being combined with the actual Sam Gordon meeting, he charged for all of that too, which was mostly defensible since while he was driving he was thinking about how he'd handle Mr. Gordon, who should have remembered that P.T. Barnum was once the mayor of Bridgeport.

Lucas was on his way out to begin another failure of the South Beach-Atkins-Weight Watchers-whatever no carb diet when the mailman came up. Another new carrier. A woman about sixty, trying to hide the grey so she didn't have to file some age discrimination suit to feed herself. Surprise, nothing good to speak of in the mail unless you count Wingy Rosenzweig rubbing it in that he was in Oahu and something from Felix Gavilan, Esq., announcing that he's relocated his offices from Atlanta proper to Peachtree City.

Rook put on his answering machine and went out to the deli for an open-faced lean corned beef on rye and a Dr. Brown. There were two phone messages when he got back to the office and somebody else's mail through the slot. Both calls were half good. Crazy Grace Savoy from across the way saying she had a fashion shoot in New Jersey for two days, did he want the job or to play hide the pickle. And Warden to say he'd call back.

Lucas spent fifteen minutes dictating his forty-eight-minute memorandum and packed up his guns for a trip to the doctor. You want to see the Tanners, you have to make an appointment like you do any other doctor. The only difference is they tell you two-thirty, they see you at two-thirty, not ten of five.

You got buzzed in to their shop on Houston Street like you were getting into Fort Knox. Armor plate door, all kinds of surveillance. Only one time did any bad guys get in and then they didn't get back out.

Maybe his eyes were going or maybe he was just bored, but more and more often, Larry Tanner wore his jeweler's loupe. And always a shirt, tie, and vest, no matter how mismatched. Francesca was in the back extracting a broken tap from a gold-fringed .45.

"You here to get the crud out?" Larry asked.

"Precisely," said Lucas.

"That's the way we do it." He turned to the back. "My love, can you put aside that garish piece of shit to accommodate our friend here?"

"Hey, Rook," she said without looking up. "You're due for an annual on your 21. You bring that too?"

"Indeed, I did."

"You leaving them both, maybe you should pick up that Bulldog Pug I've been holding for you. Bad ass piece of iron, not to mention it's a collector's item since Charter Arms went *machulla*."

"I'm good, Larry."

"You looking for a trigger enhancement, sixty-five per piece. Two for a hundred and ten."

"I'm good," said Lucas.

"Just get the crud out," said Francesca.

Lucas turned to go. "Be back tomorrow around four."

"Four-fifteen," said Larry Tanner. "Ride easy."

"Back at you," Rook told him.

He went back to the St. Claire rather than cab up to the office. There were two men with blueprints in the lobby. Not a good sign for the non-millionaires in the building, which meant most of the tenants. The only ones with serious paper were the married doctors on eight, dollars to donuts they were both banging their au pair, and the old man who was the butterfly freak. Maybe the lady who did her vaudeville bit about the building being a department store every time she got on the elevator and maybe the potted plant couple. Grace Savoy could swing it if she was banking her haute couture dollars. The rest of the building, like him, were headed to some crackerjacks box in Queens or Hoboken.

Lucas poured himself a cold one and checked his messages. There were two calls from Warden. He did not sound happy. Rook called him back.

"When you are in the employ of the Regal and/or Union Insurance Companies or any insurance company, you bind us by your actions, Mr. Rook. Do you understand that?"

"I think I do, Mr. Warden. I'm your agent. What's the problem?"

"How did you get Mr. Gordon to produce those papers?"

Rook poured the rest of his beer. "An indirect approach."

"How 'indirect'?"

"Mr. Gordon believes that Private Maguire made a binding oral will before he died."

"And that would pre-empt the assignment?"

"I'm not a lawyer, Mr. Warden. I leave that stuff up to the lawyers."

"Gordon is a lawyer, and his threats have reached all the way to the home office. And then to me."

Rook waited for him to go on.

"I'm not happy with your approach, but I can live with the results."

Lucas finished his Yuengling and eased a belch away from the receiver. "I'll handle my report accordingly."

"And the bill," said Warden. "Also I want you to hold off on any further work until you hear from me."

Rook took a breath so he wouldn't douche bag the guy. "I'm doing my job, Mr. Warden. And with good results."

"Hold off, Mr. Rook. I did not say return the file. Yet," said the insurance man and he hung up.

Lucas got to work preparing an interim report and bill. Then he called Grace. The Lord giveth, the Lord taketh away. If they were going to shitcan him on the insurance job, he'd have to spend his time watching out for his blind supermodel neighbor while she walked around half-naked.

Grace Savoy, high fashion model and diva, "blind as a bat," she always said, "but hot to trot and able to hear a pigeon fart a mile away." And nutty as a fruitcake, calling or coming over a half dozen times a day, at any time, day or night. Sometimes it was because she needed his help, like when that bird flew in off the patio, or because it was getting to her. "If only I could see how outstandingly beautiful I am, it would be of some comfort," she'd said more than a dozen times.

Grace Savoy was a good neighbor, which meant she didn't bust his balls about his being out on the patio in the middle of the night or when he was taking care of Sid Rosen, who had gotten tuned up bad in his garage. Or even when one of his bad dreams caused an AD with his Glock .21. They almost fucked a couple of times, but he knew better. You don't fuck where you eat, and right now the money she paid for him to go on the fashion shoots with her meant not having to pay a visit to the credit union while

Warden and the insurance company screwed their heads from out of their asses.

It was the second time Grace had called him since Ken Covington had died. The guy is 82nd Airborne in Nam and then PD, Border Patrol, and some congenital heart thing kills him while he's bringing Gracey home from a midnight job in Chinatown.

"On this new job in Jersey, I am not wearing a chauffeur's hat," Lucas told her. "That's one of the only two things I won't do for you, Grace Savoy. The other being picking up after your dog."

"So you will ride me like a bucking bronco and goad me with your silver spurs?"

"Goad?" he said.

"Prompt, encourage, prod. Will you prod me while you prod me?"

"Nope," he told her. "On both counts."

"Okay," she said. "You have to supply the chariot this time, neighbor."

Lucas called over to tell the gunsmiths that he'd be by a day late. He went over to Rosen's garage to pick up the limo, walking the long way to exercise his bad leg. Sid was vacuuming the back seat when Rook came in.

"You never can tell what you're going to find when one of these comes back. Condoms, bagels, once there was a live squirrel under the seat, but Bear, not this young pup, but his forefather, he got it." Sid shut down the vacuum and underhanded Lucas the car keys. "Why, once I even found a copy of some Hemingway book or whatever."

"Right, Sid. Short stories are good. Nick Adams. He was a movie star, too, right? I'm almost done. I'll get it back to you."

The new doorman was coming back down the street from walking Grace's guide dog when Rook pulled up, which meant that she'd be down when she felt like it. The doorman came over looking for a tip to let the limo wait in front, but backed off when he saw who it was. Lucas checked his watch and began to savor the literary nuances of the *Post*.

Twenty minutes passed. He called up to her apartment.

"I'm almost ready," she said. "I've got to get my scent just right to avoid any combat."

"Sure, Grace. To avoid any combat."

"So I don't do battle with the arilbred, the plicata, the..."

"Tell me about it on the way," Rook said.

"Okey dokey," she said. "I'll be right down."

They were just pulling on to 280 West for the Garden State Parkway when Grace Savoy's cell phone rang.

"No, no," she said. And she began to cry. Real tears, not the bullshit ones she did when she wanted Lucas to come over and keep her company.

"Is everything alright, Gracey?" he asked.

"The murder, the murdering fucks."

"Who, Gracey? Shall I turn around?"

She lit a cigarette and covered her blind eyes with her other hand. "The murdering fucks. It's the diaspora all over again."

"You want me to take you back or go ahead to Montclair for your shoot?"

She was sobbing now. "The holocaust, Lucas. I want you to get the fuckers. 'Remember and Avenge.'"

Rook pulled over to the side of the road. "What's going on, Grace? Is somebody dead?"

"The assignment is. And terrorists. I want you to get them."

Lucas turned the radio on.

"No, Lucas Rook. More than a hundred rare irises, some dating back to the 1500's, stomped, slashed, crushed at Memorial Gardens, where the shoot was to be. Ms. Meyers said the Montclair Police are there, but they'll never catch them. And besides, what does it matter?" She snubbed out her menthol and lit another.

"Chief Sabagh knows his stuff, and the Essex County Detectives can run a case."

"Will you get the fuckers, Lucas Rook? I'll have the Gardens or the Iris Society retain you or I'll pay you myself."

Lucas got back onto the road. "We'll see, Grace. In the meantime, there's a jug handle up ahead. You want me to go back to the City, this job is dead?"

"Please don't use that word just now, Lucas. And besides, we get paid anyway, 'Act of God, *force majeure*.' Take me home. I may be blind, but I'm not stupid."

The way Warren G. Phelps, Esquire, explained it, it's more putting the rabbit into the hat than pulling it out. He pulls the rabbit out of the hat when the US Attorney is happy he's got better things to do than roust Lucas Rook for blasting two jacketed rounds into a cop-killer's head. Then there's the artistry when Phelps bills you so it makes perfect sense that he's working forty hours a day and you're happy to pay him what you make a week for one of those magic hours.

So now Lucas Rook knows the art about how there's time and then there's *time* and when you're billing somebody who knows the game like a decent insurance adjuster does, you got to make your bill read like one of those Philip K. Dick books that Sid Rosen gave him, *Time Out of Joint* or whatever. Everett Warden says no more billing, you got to get in as much as you can backwards so that nobody with a decent computer program can make your magic tricks look like mail fraud.

Detective Graves is going to talk to him, and no way he's going to talk to the insurance company about when and if he talked to Rook. That means a half day's billing, including the write-up for what hasn't happened yet, which meant he'd better reach out for that interview pronto. Even at the insurance company's shitty hourly rates, it wasn't chump change, particularly if the job was irretrievably flushed.

Dwight Graves could be a halfway surly prick and had treated him like somebody who didn't know any better when him and Hy Gromek were looking at grabbing the jitbag who beat Rosen. But two shots of good liquor would get Detective Graves' mouth moving, even if it was about how Hy was dead and so was Kirk and how the job sucked anyway, especially for a black man. That mouth moving was the meter running.

Dwight said Miata's was as good a place as any other, particularly since somebody else was buying. When Rook got there, DG was sitting at the bar, dressed as Hollywood as ever with a grey suit and black turtleneck. The beard was new.

Dobie or Obie, one of the two wiseasses, poured Graves his first Crown Royal and Lucas a Jack and water. "*Fidelis ad mortem,*" toasted Graves. Rook nodded.

"The whiskers new?" Lucas asked.

"Got to keep folks from thinking I'm Bill Cosby the way he's got himself in the shit." He drank his drink and tapped the glass for another. "The boy should have kept his millionaire mouth closed about what's wrong in the black community."

"Thought you had gone Muslim or whatever," Lucas said.

"You always were a funny man, Rook. What can I do for you?"

Lucas put a Churchill Sumatra up on the bar.

Graves sniffed the cigar and put it in his pocket.

"You bring me a box of these, you got somebody you want dead?"

"I'm good, Dwight." Lucas sipped his drink. "So how's Pauline doing?"

"She's just getting through it since Hy died. One reason I never married." His refill arrived. "You buying me a steak dinner, you can ask me the other reason."

"No expense account for that, but here's alright. Let's grab a table."

The waitress came over. Fat Girl trying to turn that into nice tits. Lucas ordered the roast beef sandwich on a kaiser roll. Graves told the girl he wanted shrimp in the basket.

"That's why," he said when she walked away.

"Why what?"

"Why I never married. At least half the reason. Junk in the trunk."

Rook called to junk in the trunk for another Jack Daniels.

"The other reason, Lucas Rook, is I don't want my old lady winding up like Hy's did. Or your sister-in-law." He finished his Crown Royal.

"Helen Maguire," Lucas said. "I'm working for the insurance company."

"Right, right. Irish lady, must have been pretty once. She drank a lot. They all do. Takes a header down the steps. She's dead."

"The fall kill her?"

"Probably. Although maybe she choked on her own blood and vomit, there was a lot of that."

The waitress brought their meals. Lucas sent her back for the onion.

"Anything about the splatter pattern or whatever?" Rook asked.

Detective Graves tucked a napkin in his turtleneck and dipped a shrimp into the cocktail sauce. "Only thing about the blood was some smudges on the wall which most likely was Crime Scene not being as tidy as they are on television.

"I hate that shit anyway. Saw what's-his-name Petersen of CSI in a picture the other night. Bit part in *Thief*. That was a movie. James Caan." Graves dipped another shrimp. "Anyway, her blood alcohol was inconsistent with her being falling down drunk." Graves patted the pocket the cigar was in. "You need copies of the reports?"

"Yesterday would be good. The canvas, 61's, whatever?"

DG ate another shrimp. "French fries are poison. Nothing to

speak of. I had her brother in. Half a wiseguy. Used to run with the Westies. Spent some time inside, but he's nothing. There was talk she had a boyfriend. Maybe more."

"You got a name?"

"I got to be going, Rook. Pleasure dining with you. Hear they got fine aged steaks over at Arthur's."

Graves left without shaking hands. Rook let him get up and leave. If the insurance company takes his balls out of their vise and the job is back on, Dwight Graves can have his steak. Otherwise, it's mac and cheese and who gives a shit.

A fine-looking pros walked by as Lucas finished his sandwich. Nice approach, the college girl-look, sweater and whatnot, but probably the ladies room is the only thing ever going to be lady-like about her. A lot of talk now about the escort service business, housewives, college students with steady customers. Right. "Honey, I'm home. I'll have that meatloaf in the oven for you and the kids in just a jiffy, just let me get rid of this cock breath."

The hooker came back after douching herself or whatever.

"Buy you a drink with an umbrella in it?" Lucas asked her.

She did one of those hair-flips and gave a Vassar smile. "I don't think so," she said.

"That cop smell coming off of me is retired, honey, but that's alright. I probably couldn't afford you."

Another Vassar smile as she fingered her pearls. "Probably not," she said.

Rook left a five for the waitress and two singles for Obie-Dobie and went back into the New York night. Still nothing like it, the night saying that the City is still happening. The towel heads going to have to keep coming back, maybe fifty times before the action, the smartness is going to stop. Probably it never will. Too much going on, too many presents being bought, too many deals being made, which is not to say that all these New York lights and taxis going by with rich folks in expensive clothes were going to do him any good.

What was cooking for him was Hamburger Helper unless Everett Warden gave him the okay to get the insurance job running again. In the meantime, he'd make some calls to see if anything was up. Ryan, the attorney from Long Island. The Felix Gavilan show. The Park Avenue firm of Kipps, Wetherill, and Hobbes. Maybe even the scumbucket who had him on the little run to Florida to get the paper signed. Then there was the odds and ends for Grace. She'd get him a check for the job in the gardens that got cancelled. Also see if any of the esteemed colleagues in his line of work had anything they couldn't handle or needed to lay off.

It was too late to get much of anybody on the phone except Owlsie. Owls Miksis kept late hours and with age gaining on him, he more and more had a piece on his plate that he could share.

"Excelsior Investigations," answered Owls.

"Still keeping the nighttime hours, Owlsie?"

"Is that you, Lucas Rook? What can I do you for?"

"Looking for some subwork," Rook told him.

"Things slow, Lucas. All them big companies and the pretenders whatnot using the internet to steal our clients. Used to be, the only net in our line of work was the one thrown over the bad guys." He stifled a yawn. "Unless you're counting *Dragnet,* the TV show and all. Met Jack Webb once. Nice guy. Pissing shame he smoked himself to death, which reminds me," Miksis lit a cigarette. "But I may have something. That fancy lawyer, Phelps, called me for some spadework for Izzy Frelang's kid, Shirl, who runs the newsstand. You interested, the running around is not too compatible with my edema, me retaining fluid the way I am."

"Well, you just put them legs up on your fancy desk, Owls, let gravity do its work, but I got to pass on that. You get anything else, give me a buzz."

It was not a good thing to give up work, especially now, but no way could he handle the Shirl Frelang job. She's jammed up over selling untaxed smokes, she calls him, he sends her to Warren Phelps, who sends the work to Miksis. Warren Phelps is smart

enough to know that Shirl's talking to him first is not protected by
any attorney-client privilege. If it was just him and not Phelps he'd
work it out. Especially when the cupboard's bare. But you don't jam
up your lawyer anymore than you slam the door on your own dick.

Rook hailed a taxi. The Arab driver trying to pass for Mexican.
Muhammad tried a "*Gracias*" when Lucas handed over the fare and
a buck tip, but got a "*Shalom*" back at him. Lucas thought about
stopping for a couple of cold ones, but the way things were going it
was going to have to be Chez Fridge to end the day.

The new deskman was dozing. At least some things didn't
change, at least not yet. These architects with their plans under the
arm were going to be converting the building sooner or later. And
unless he got things going 360, there was nothing he was going to
be able to even think about other than the pull-out couch in the office. Maybe an apartment in Queens. Artie Carlin said the council-
woman owned a couple of buildings that were alright and she'd
probably be glad to have him as a tenant.

There was a note from Grace Savoy under Rook's apartment
door. Blind from birth, but with penmanship that would make any
nun proud. Lucas poured himself a cold one and changed his shoes.
His leg wasn't getting any worse, but it wasn't getting any better, and
more and more it was getting to his feet. Dr. Zarro was a magician,
but you're doing PI business you can't wear shoes that make you
look like a gym teacher.

Grace let him in her apartment. She was pacing back and forth
so that her guide dog was flipping out.

"The IRF has a fund. They need you," she said. "It's genocide."

"The IRA, you mean, Grace. I don't…"

"No, Lucas Rook." She lit a cigarette with the one burning in
the ashtray. "Not them. The Iris Restoration Fund. A good retainer. People are saying it was the developers who want to put in
townhouses where the Memorial Gardens are."

"It's not for me, Grace."

She walked another set of the geometric patterns in her head, to the door and back and then around the couch.

"They should put in motion sensors, security cameras, a fence," Lucas told her.

"They're going to do that, but not the fence. I spoke to them. But this is more than that. If they can't figure out which species is which or if the plants can't withstand the shock and stress, the genetic lines will be lost forever."

He stepped towards her, but she sensed his movement and retreated. "Never mind, Lucas Rook," she said. "You go back to whatever you do. Working for scumbags is for you, Lucas Rook. Working for scumbags and working for me, seeing me naked. That's for you, Lucas. That's all."

9

Downtime was bad time for Lucas Rook. If he had retainer clients, which he didn't, things would be different. Go fishing off of Montauk, fly out to Vegas, or sit home and toast the Jets trying to pretend they were the Giants. And all the while the meter was running. Now it meant following up on those calls that he hadn't already been told nothing's doing and drawing down on his bank account.

He went over to Tanner's to pick up his Glocks and shoot the shit with Larry, maybe shoot for beers. Three or four boxes of wadcutters for a pitcher of beer and a crabcake sandwich, unless Francesca felt moved to get in it, in which case she outshot them both.

Lucas was lucky that she was busy in a screaming match with the rep from Last Chance about how they were shorted in their last order of vests. Larry's bad finger was bothering him, like what happened to Koufax, he liked to say, so it was just the beer.

"She's a pisser, ain't she, Rook? Knew the first time I met her. She was teaching school over in Barrington." He took the last onion ring. "I tell you Julie's going to vet school? Something, isn't it, her mother wouldn't let anything in the house that didn't wipe its feet on the mat and she's going to be a veterinarian."

They had had that conversation maybe five times before. Rook looked at his watch. Nothing else was doing, so maybe he'd be going out to see Tuzio at the policemen's home. Doing that twice in a week will fuck up their schedule of when not to be neglecting Tuze. He went over to get the car.

Rosen was bringing a Ford Escape off the lift. "Uncle Sam says you drive a hybrid, they're going to give you a tax credit, Lucas. You're going to ask me what I think of that, aren't you, Lucas boy? Well, it's the government getting involved in business, which they shouldn't. The lefties inviting Dracula in, although they don't know it."

"Just what I was going to talk to you about, Sidney. Bela Lugosi. That and would you get Kirk's car ready? I'm going to run out and see Tuze."

The garageman wiped his handprints off the steering wheel. "Going to take him that book I lent you?"

"I'm almost done with it, Sid."

"Lugosi's last wish was to be buried in his Dracula cape. Did you know that?" asked Rosen.

"I did not know that, Sid. Going over to Joe's while you bring the Avanti out."

The garageman wiped his hands again. "See if he'll give you what's too old for the stew pot for Bear."

"Will do," said Rook.

He walked over to the restaurant, coming up the alley to go in the back door. Sam was arguing with a hip-hop and getting in his face pretty good.

"You nothing but a smart mouth dressed up like a clown, Kenneth."

"My name's Jamar, Unc. And Shamaka's nothing but a biscuit head."

The cook moved in close. "She only fourteen."

"She don't be banging boots like she no fourteen, Unc."

"You disrespecting the girl and yourself."

The teenager pulled on his neck chain and posed. "I be craculating, Pops."

Sam grabbed him. "I be craculating your nappy head, nephew. Now get on down the road. I hear from your aunt again, you're going to see this old man dance and you're not going to like it."

Jamar stepped back. "Now with your permission," he said, "I'm going to bizounce."

"He be disrespecting my place of business," Sam said as Rook arrived.

"Not a good thing, Samuel."

"No it isn't. Good thing is I'm about to cook up some of yesterday's pot roast on the grill. Fried up some onions, seasoned rice. Glass of buttermilk."

"If that's an invitation, I'm sitting down," said Rook.

Sam worked the grill, drawing a figure eight with the oil and scrambling the rice and onions while the meat sizzled.

"Joe around?" Rook asked.

"He took Jeanie over to the Fashion Institute."

Sam plated the meat and seasoned rice and poured them each a glass of buttermilk. Then he put down a stack of white bread and buttered up some slices. "I remember when we had bread sandwiches and were happy for it, and I don't mean back home. I mean Joe and me." He said a little grace, then started eating. "Time has its own way," he said. And they finished their meal without another word.

"Sid asked you have anything for his dog, Samuel," Lucas said.

"It's for that dog of his, I got mashed potatoes with mashed potatoes. That dog eat better than both of us do." He went over to the stock pot and spooned out some of the potatoes and carrot pieces. "Used to be he ate my cooking himself until him and Joe had that set-to. Talking about the war never got anybody anywhere."

The cook poured the last of the buttermilk. "I put aside some cobbler."

"Appreciate it, Samuel, but I got to run. Next time I'm making the meal."

"Not in my kitchen you ain't. Meanwhile, you take the dessert for later."

Rook took the bowl of food for Rosen and the cobbler for Ray Tuzio and went back over to the garage. There was a note on the door, "Gone for parts," which could mean Sid took a trip to the salvage yard, a nap in the back, or even to the Chinese woman around the corner to keep his plumbing working.

Lucas used his key. His twin brother's black fiberglass coupe was up front. The black Avanti made a good rumble coming out of the pipes and no way was he selling what was his brother's. Sid had asked him a couple of times and it was tempting, particularly when the forty-some-year-old car needed parts and the cash flow was bad like it was now, but the only time he'd consider selling it was when he was flat broke and that hadn't happened yet.

Lucas was halfway out to the Policemen's Home when the steering went to shit. He pulled over to the side and called Rosen on his cell. The garageman picked it up on the sixth ring. "Steering's shot, Sid."

"We just put in new valves. That Bendix kit isn't worth shit."

A yellow tow truck pulled over. "Anybody hurt?" the driver asked.

"You running accident cases, I got nothing for you, pal," Lucas told him.

"You get some personal injury, you call my lawyer here." He tried handing over a card, but Rook let it drop. "You got body work, I'll hook you up too."

Rook tinned him. "You want a straight run back into the City, you got it. Otherwise, have a nice day."

The tow truck pulled away.

Rosen called back. "You want me to come get you or see if I can get somebody closer? Either way is good, but don't be trying to drive back here, just turning left or whatever. Give me fifteen minutes."

Rook got some downshifting gawkers and then another tow pulled up. The driver was a big black woman with a red leather cap. "Sidney says to bring you in. Hop on up, while I hook you up. Name is Starr, two R's."

She secured the Avanti and climbed back into the cab. "You mind if I smoke?" she said as she fired up a Newport. "It's my rig, but I figure you're my guest up in here."

"I'm good," Rook said.

"I bet you are, honey," she told him.

They listened to Motown on the way back and swapped jokes and flirtations which neither of them meant. When they got to the garage, Rook handed over his driver's club info and one of his business cards with the chess piece on it.

"Ooh," she said. "And you can protect me too." Another call came over her radio and she took a wreck on the east side.

Rook went back to the St. Claire. More activity in the lobby, which meant they were looking more and more to go condo.

He checked his messages. One from the Police Benevolent Association asking for money to support keeping the cops' Bill of Rights in the union contract. And one from Everett Warden. Rook called him back.

"You're back on," the insurance man said. "Marshall Funding filed suit. I don't particularly like the way you handled things up to now. Maybe that's even why the shyster is suing, but he didn't even give me the courtesy of a phone call. So the liar, I mean lawyer, gets what he deserves. Full court press, Rook. But watch the billing. I will be."

The day was no longer shit on a stick. Lucas opened himself a can of Yuengling and called the garage.

"I got good news and bad news," said Rosen.

"Will I be able to tell the difference, Sid?"

"Good is, there's not a scratch on the vehicle. The lady sure can drive. Bad news, if the Bendix kit isn't defective, it will be time to open up the pocketbook again. You know I can always get

$22,500 or so. There's that buyer calls me now and then from York, and we can always list it in *Hemmings*."

"Let me know what the damage is, Sid. I'm still thinking it's something I want to hold on to."

10

Now that the Maguire job was up, if Dwight Graves wanted a
steak at Arthur's to pass along what else he had on Helen Maguire's
boyfriend, he got it. The bill for DG's cooperation was too much to
submit to the client, it would get charged some other way.

Lucas got Dwight's voicemail on the cell, sounding half badass, half Sidney Poitier. He tried over to the squad. Lichty answered.
He was a good guy. His older brother was retired off the job and he
was getting close.

"Detective Graves is not present. May I be of assistance?" he
said.

"You trying to jump his play being all polite and whatnot?"
Rook said.

"Who's this?"

"Somebody helped your big brother wipe your nose. Doody
said you always had your finger in it."

Lichtenfeld thought for a while. "Well, this got to be Lucas
Rook, arch crime fighter and 'captain of industry.'"

Lucas took out a 3x5 card in case he got anything. "Correct,
young man. How you treating the world?"

Lichty put him on hold and then got back on. "The boss is

squeezing my shoes. But what do you expect from an empty suit, pencil head. Today is DG's RDO. Something I can help you with?"

"Helen Maguire."

"Don't know that job, Lucas. I'll tell him you called. Meanwhile, I got to go pretend I give a crap."

Rook noted both phone calls and sorted through his pile of bills now that he knew that there was a likelihood that he was going to pay them.

The phone rang. "Mr. Rook, my name is Wilhelm Tschoeppe. The 'T' is silent. I need your assistance."

Rook took out another index card.

"I'm with the Iris Society. That's the flower, not Ireland."

"I'm familiar with your situation, Mr. Tschoeppe. I understand that the Montclair police are hard at work, and I believe there's a restoration fund to get the garden back together."

Tschoeppe cleared his throat. "That is the Iris Restoration Fund. That's an ad hoc group. We're a national group, international actually." He cleared his throat again. "And we are interested in retaining you."

"Regarding the tearing up of Memorial Gardens?"

"It's more than that. If you'll meet with me, we'll pay for the initial consultation."

"I am actually pretty well booked." He could hear the puff of a bronchial inhaler and the deep breath to take the medicine in.

"The Iris Society is quite well-funded for this project," said Tschoeppe. "A handsome endowment was recently made for this purpose with the express condition that you be retained."

"My astute detective skills lead me to believe it emanated from somewhere in my fair city. In fact, I can probably describe the donor."

"I'm not at liberty to discuss that. May we schedule that consultation now?"

Lucas looked at his calendar and his office. Even with his office building being refurbished, the décor was still undeniably "low rent." Low rent means low fees, and while this job wasn't going anywhere past the initial meeting, there was no reason to advertise what he didn't have.

"The Waldorf lobby, tomorrow at eleven. I have a half hour between meetings."

"I'm afraid that's not possible, my asthma and these allergies being what they are. We're in Laurel Springs, New Jersey, not North Carolina." Another dose of the atomizer. "Actually, Walt Whitman used to come here for his health. There's a joke there." Tschoeppe coughed. "We've been directed to pay you up to a thousand dollars for your services."

"I can do that," said Rook.

Even though it was just a run down the Turnpike, Lucas did some spadework, which thanks to technology meant some time on the Internet. There hadn't been much crime in Laurel Springs for years, although there was a murder shoot-out over a woman on Labor Day 2005. The town had a couple of thousand residents. The police station was in the former Gray Stone Mansion. Michael Walcott was chief. He didn't know him, but Jersey Joe Walcott was born Arnold Cream and won the heavyweight title when he was 37. Knocked Joe Lewis down, refereed the Clay-Liston "phantom punch" fight and got leveled by the greatest right hand in history by Rocky Marciano.

Rook did a quick Mapquest to refresh his memory, which was only that Laurel Springs was about fifteen miles from Philly and about a mile from the amusement park. He picked up the Merc from Rosen's garage and made good time except for the usual Exit 7 bottleneck. Then a jog onto Route 73 and 295 to the White Horse Pike, which used to be something before the AC Expressway: decent diners, cheap gas, the produce stands. Heaven for Jimbo Turner to see all the bushel baskets of sweet corn and real Jersey tomatoes.

Lucas took down the miles off the odometer and parked across the street from the two-story white building. The lawn was manicured, the iron fence freshly painted white. There were flowers all around. A tasteful sign on the front door indicated the Iris Society was on the first floor. Lucas rang the bell.

"I'm around the back, through the second gate," said Tschoeppe. "Watch the dog."

Rook took his ankle piece and put it in his jacket pocket and went to the rear yard. There was a golden retriever lying in the flower bed. Tschoeppe had his back turned and was lining up a fairly long putt.

"Your dog's in the flowers," Rook said.

"Shhh," said the iris man. "It's sudden death." He stroked the ball well, then walked towards his miss to tap it in. "Doctor does that. Doctor's the dog's name. He knows not to move a muscle while I'm putting." He tapped it in and picked up his ball. "Golf's a passion," he said.

Lucas thought about the line he had thrown at the accountant on the Janice Scheyman job, "I don't think you should hit anything that isn't going to try and hit you back," but let it go.

"Golf and flowers. Irises in particular," Tschoeppe said as he turned around. His face was scarred. His nose reconstructed. His eyes were slits.

"A blind golfer with terrible allergies who loves flowers. Quite the ironies." He reached out his hand and walked toward Rook's voice.

The dog ran over.

"And a guide dog who's a song and dance man. Now that I've won the Master's again with my two-putt, let's go inside and I'll pour us a drink. Beer, I would guess. Most boxers like beer and you have boxer's hands."

"Very observant, Mr. Tschoeppe."

"Call me Will, if you would. 'Will the Thrill,' our Grace used to call me. We went to 'blind school' together at the Wade Institute. 'The blind leading the blind,' we used to say. 'Dis-Grace' she wanted to be known as, but I could never bring myself to do that."

He led the way into the white building. It was completely residential except for a work area in the alcove.

"Work," he told the dog. The retriever came over and sat down. "Grab us a couple of cold ones, Doctor." Wilhelm Tschoeppe sat down and kicked off his shoes. "Actually, I'm a beer man too. The perfect chaser for my allergy meds. People think you run the Iris Society, you like white wine or something. That's not necessarily so. In fact, some of us are quite rough actually. Alec Fisher is president of the South African chapter and is career military."

The retriever made his deliveries. Wilhelm handed Rook his beer and poured some into the palm of his hand for the dog.

"So here goes," he said. "We're a non-profit formed in 1957, a breakaway group from the Philadelphia chapter. There's all kinds of rivalry. The biologists, the gardeners, us." Tschoeppe cleared his throat. "Basically, you have your three main 'categories' of iris, let's call them. Bearded, non-bearded, Aril. There's around three hundred different species. You ask me, there's 296. Your bearded have bushy beards on the falls, that's the lower petals. We've got standard, intermediate, boarder, and miniature."

He took a long pull on his beer. "You've got your beardless which mostly come from Asia. There's your Siberian, Japanese, PCN's, CA's. Used to be you had your Louisianas, very nice signal crests. Then you got your Aril, no 'p,' which are divided into your oncocycles and your regalia. Great colors, but hard to grow around here."

Tschoeppe finished his beer and put the bottle on the ground. The dog came over and carried it to a trash can in the corner. "We recycle here," he said.

"You examine an iris, you check the raffling and the lacing, the horns and the spoons. There are diploids and tetraploids. Ancestors are called pod parents and pollen parents. I lost my sight making a rocket to the moon on my twelfth birthday."

Lucas put his empty down and the dog retrieved.

"Do you have any questions, Mr. Rook?"

"What particular services do you have in mind?"

Tschoeppe went over to his desk and came back with an envelope. "Monitor the case, keep me informed, coordinate with the authorities if there's information to pass on. That kind of thing at your usual rate for the period the retainer will cover."

Rook got up. "Grace Savoy writes you five, ten, whatever. You give me a grand for doing nothing. The difference goes into your pocket. A blind man can see that, Willie."

"As I told you, they are the Society's funds. I'll be happy to bring the matter up at the next monthly meeting."

"Grace Savoy is a friend of mine, Billy boy. So right now you're a quorum or whatever and you just had an emergency meeting and you're going to refund it all. And if you're wondering if I'd beat a blind man, the answer is yes."

Wilhelm went over to his desk and wrote another check. Then he inhaled a dose of his asthma medicine. "Don't let the door hit you in the ass on the way out, Mr. Rook," he said.

11

Lucas Rook drove back to New York—"back up the turn-pike," Salerno from the Philly PD used to say. Worst thing is for a cop to die in the streets like Salerno did, unless maybe it's your twin brother for which you get there only in time to see him bleeding out on the sidewalk. They all got it who had shot Kirk down like a dog, Etillio, all of them.

"Thanks for nothing," he said out loud as he drove past the exit for Catherine Wren's house. Maybe another week or so they'd get back together again if he'd wake up Prince Charming and not half a surly prick headbanger. Right. And elephants fly. Lucas fiddled with the radio and then convinced himself to call. He got Catherine's machine, but halfway through her message, she picked up.

A camper driven by an old guy with a much younger woman drifted into his lane.

"Keep your eye on the road instead of her knish," Lucas yelled.

"I love when you talk sweet to me," said Catherine.

"Not you, Cat."

"Of course not. Where are you?"

"On the scenic New Jersey Turnpike. How about we get some

takeout burritos and we play chimichanga under the blanket?"

"There's a new place just opened in Princeton. 'Viva Miguel.' I'd like you to take me there."

"Ole," he told her and hung up before she could say no.

Lucas got off the Turnpike and waited in line to pay the toll. EZ Pass saves time, but then the world knows where you've been and when.

Catherine Wren was waiting outside when he got to her house. Cashmere sweater, sensible shoes, looking just like the professor that she was.

"So you meet me outside so I'm sure not to grab for any appetizer or whatnot?"

She looked at her watch. "We're going to be late as it is, and getting a reservation was almost impossible." She kissed him on the cheek.

"Show me the way to this new fancy Mexican joint that doesn't do takeout." Lucas held the car door for her. Their joke. She waited for him to close it, so she could open it up for herself.

There was a line outside of Viva Miguel's.

"See?" she said.

"I don't see a wetback in the bunch. Good Mexican, Chinese, Jap food, whatever, their own kind eat there."

Catherine Wren took his hand and they walked to the head of the line.

"We're ahead of you," said a *Soprano*-wannabe type in an open shirt and lots of gold.

Lucas ignored him.

"We have reservations," said Catherine.

"So do we," said the wannabe. "So back of the line."

Rook leaned in and said something, then took Catherine's arm and went inside.

"Right this way, Dr. Wren," said the hostess.

"You got pull here, huh, Dr. Wren?" said Rook.

"Claudine's in one of my classes, which is how I heard about this place. Poor dear, she's been trying to graduate for ten or eleven years or something."

Catherine ordered a Margarita Hamilton, which was black and green. Lucas had a Corona.

"I have to drink it fast," Catherine said when her drink arrived. "*It's melting.*"

"I don't get it."

"Margarita Hamilton, the witch in the Wizard of Oz, '*I'm melting.*'"

Rook started his beer. "That explains the rest of the drinks on the menu. Margarita Thatcher, Ann Margarita, Margarita Cho, I guess that's made with tuna fish or something."

"That's not right. Besides, with many of these girls, it's just a phase, 'lugs' they call them."

"Isn't that a kind of shoe?"

"Lesbian Until Graduation."

"That's nice, Catherine. 'Hi, honey, how's classes? Swell, Daddy, I got a B in dildos and a B+ in Carpet Munching.'"

Catherine Wren put down her margarita. "That's not nice talk, Lucas. I thought you were working on that. Which reminds me, what did you say to that man in line?"

Rook picked up his menu. "I told him in the joint John Gotti pulled out his implants with a pliers from the shoe repair."

"Why would he do that?"

"Looking for a radio transmitter, whatever. Throat and mouth cancer didn't help much. I hear the Dapper Don was lucky if he got a Tylenol. Now let's eat. I wonder if they have something with beans and cheese?"

Rook had steak fajitas. Catherine had something with cilantro. They went back to her house with the lilac bushes outside the windows and the gazebo in the back.

"Will you come in for coffee?" she asked. "You see I don't have my foot in the door."

"I will," he said. "Is that morning coffee?"

"Perhaps."

"One minute," Lucas told her. "I almost forgot." He went back to the car for the bunch of blue irises that he had taken from Wilhelm Tschoeppe's yard.

Rook's phone rang the next morning on the way up the turn-pike. It was Dwight Graves returning the call.

"You got something for me?" Lucas said.

"My physician says I've got iron poor blood. He prescribed prime rib. Only if you want to do this, we got to do it today. One-thirty. I've got other plans for the dinner hour."

Arthur's was at the old Maxwell's Plum, a famous pick-up joint in the '60s. That was then. The joint got cannibalized by the credi-tors and then the auction house so now the bar from Maxwell's was in the Tribeca Grill, while the Looking For Mr. Goodbar chicks who used to lean on it were probably at the plastic surgeon for the third time around.

Lucas was at the steak place ten minutes early. For any cop worth a damn, on time meant being early. Except, of course, if you're a black cop trying to teach whitey a lesson. Detective Graves rolled up twenty minutes late. Rook had been around the block a couple of times and in the drugstore across the way so that he wasn't drawing attention.

"Sorry to keep you waiting, Rook," he said. "You know how it is."

They both did. The Scotty dogs turning on the glass like Hy Gromek had said or some similar shit.

"I'm good, Dwight. Appreciate your making time."

Graves opened the door for him to get in.

"Got something on Helen's boyfriend. The flame was gone, but they saw each other from time to time. Could even put him in the timeframe you're looking at. Could also be the lovely, red-headed, freckle-faced Helen Maguire was giving it up to an African man. They had what you call a 'stormy relationship.' Society and all, no doubt."

"Could be, Dwight? I don't get the 'could.' "

"What I'm telling you, Rook, in respect for your brother and for this exquisite surf and turf dinner I'm about to enjoy solo, I give you all I got. African ancestry, tan complexion, black, close-cropped hair. Boy's name is D'Angelo Anthony. Got that and more too." Graves smoothed his lapels. "The two lovebirds had a love child."

"You got specifics?" Lucas asked.

"Your boy relocated to the West Coast. No way NYPD's paying for me to travel any further than the city limits on this job. Best I got, he works at this Italian joint. Here's the last known."

"Hearty appetite, DG," Rook said. "And you sure do resemble Bill Cosby."

They shook hands, exchanging the address for President Grant.

Lucas went back to his office at 166 Fifth Avenue. The super was arguing with one of the girls from the ad agency about smoking in the building.

"The vestibule is part of the building, dear. And since this is a smoke-free building, you can't smoke in the vestibule, Melissa. It's as simple as that."

"It's as simple as you can go fuck yourself, Manny. How's that?"

"Now, now, girls," Lucas told him on his way by. "Let's not get our panties in a knot."

Lucas went up to his office as another temp mail carrier came down the hall. This time it was a tall skinny white boy with streaked hair. He had earphones on and was finger-popping his way down the hall. The mail was halfway wrong, some for down the hall, some for upstairs.

"Hey, Vanilla Ice, whatever," Rook called, but it was too late.

Rook checked his messages. A call from Gracey, one from Warden and Mrs. Tanner calling that his office supplies were ready. How quaint and concerned you describe a pair of Glocks like they're paper and pens or whatnot. Her voice always had that sexy quality. He'd call her back last, an antidote to the bullshit that he was going to get from Grace Savoy behind the way his meeting with the flowerman went.

Lucas lubricated his vocal cords with a cold one and dialed Everett Warden. "Checking in, boss," Rook gave him.

"You have something?" Warden asked.

"I just met with the homicide detective who ran the Helen Maguire case. The good news is we've come up with a boyfriend and that they had a kid. Another beneficiary, it looks like, which could turn things around, I think. The bad thing is it looks like he's in San Francisco."

"I like that," said Warden. "Let me run some numbers, Rook. I'll call you back in fifteen minutes."

Just enough time to deal with Grace's hysterics. Do it wrong and you've got a crazy lady living next door with a vendetta for you, and any future work on her modeling shoots is out the window. Fortunately, he got her machine. Today she was being Billie Jean King announcing that she had just beat the balls off of Bobby Riggs.

He left her a message. "This is Rook, Gracey. Your Iris Society guy was a fraud. I got your five grand back. I'll talk to the Montclair police and see what I can do to help them out. And you go, girl, way to rush the net."

Everett Warden called back in exactly fifteen minutes. "I'll make the travel arrangements, you won't like them, plus a cap of a grand for this new beneficiary piece, including report. Take it or leave it. A penny more makes it worth it to hire somebody out there. Get me out a bill tomorrow for everything before this call, I'll process it today."

"What about expenses?"

"You get fifty dollars per diem for meals. I want receipts. And bring me back something."

There was a knock at Rook's apartment door. Then rapping, which meant it had to be Grace Savoy. Sometimes she did Poe's *The Raven*, or music, like show tunes which he didn't get, and lately it was Morse code.

"It's code for 'You're a mean crusty prick' and I'm going to keep saying it until you tell me that you're sorry," Grace said.

"I guess we're talking about my visit with your old school chum, Wilhelm, Gracey. But he's a thief and I got your money back."

"He was going to rob me *blind*, you were going to say, weren't you?"

"Nope."

"You could have let me handle it, Lucas. I'm not *crippled*, am I? Anyway, I spoke to the police chief like you said and they're 'on top of it.' Speaking of that, would you like to come next door and get on top of me? And before you answer, I have a lingerie shoot under the Washington Square arch the day after tomorrow. Can you drive me?"

Rook got back up. "You got a trifeca, Grace Savoy. No-no-no. I'll be out of town for a couple of days. You have any emergencies that can't wait, call Joe Oren or Sid at the garage."

She lit the cigarette that she had been fiddling with. "You going on vacation, Lucas? Anyplace exotic?"

He walked her to the door. "Work, Gracey, and I'm going to San Fran."

"Oh," she said. "San Francisco. That explains why you won't get on top of me." Grace took a double-hit of menthol smoke. "You're really quite a dear, Lucas, trying to get my money back. But so is Wilhelm actually. I'm sure he would have put it to good use. Which reminds me, are you sure you won't get on top of me?"

"If you need me, Gracey, use my cell."

She started across the hall to her apartment. "If it's because I'm like your sister, that's not necessarily all bad. We could really do that."

"Great. That's just what I want to hear," Lucas said.

When Grace was back across the hall, he called the Tanners. Francesca answered.

"I'm with a customer," she said.

"It's Rook. I'm coming over. Everything okay?"

"Peachy. If I put the broom up my ass I could sweep the place. Give me a half to catch up."

Lucas walked slow over to the gun shop and stopped on the way at Loren's Coffee Shop. By this time of day the donuts would only be okay, but the coffee was always decent. Loren had a Mets cap on, which probably meant he was making another run at hair-plugs.

"Long time no see," Loren said. "Joe Oren let you escape to come over here. I'll keep my thumb out your cup for this special occasion. Try the apple crumb, the sinkers is shot."

"You're the boss," Lucas said. "How's things?"

"Doing good, doing good." He leaned in close. "They're coming back at me for the third time about buying the building, the developer is. I got them on a string."

"That's good." Lucas took a forkful of the cake. "So's the

apple crumb."

"Appreciate that you don't call it 'Jewish apple cake.' I hate that, 'Jewish pickle, Jewish rye.' What do they think we do all day?"

Rook ate some more of the cake and finished his coffee. He reached for his wallet.

"Your money's no good here. Never was since you and Kirk kept me from being dead." He leaned in again. "And I appreciate you're not saying anything about me wearing this hat, which means I'm still trying to get my hair back." Loren started to take off his cap, then stopped. "They call the new process 'reanimation.' It still hurts like a bitch and costs me plenty."

"Take it light," Lucas told him. "I'll tell Joe Oren he ever wants to take a coffee break to come on over."

"I appreciate that, Rook. I do. Come on by for breakfast or lunch, whatever. No way am I ever going to think you're trying to Masterbadge me."

The customer coming out of the Tanners' gunshop was either Lee Ermey or somebody who looked just like him. Francesca buzzed Rook in. She was in the shop by herself.

"Not a pretty sight, is it?" she said. "Woman of my radiant blonde beauty wearing an apron, rubber gloves and a magnifier."

"Not to mention the understated tee-shirt, 'Guns Don't Kill People, I Do!' Nice touch."

She slid the jeweler's loupe up to her head. "You see that movie star just left? We get all the pistoleros in here, real and otherwise. What can I do you for?"

"My Glocks, to get the crud out. Larry took them."

"Right, right. He tried to sell you a trig job." She looked at her book.

"They were ready yesterday," she said.

"I wasn't. Larry alright?"

"Today's his dialysis day and I'm up to my ass in alligators."

She went back to the gun vault. "Larry says you had pastrami, sauerkraut all up in there." She laughed at her own joke. "You in the market, I've got some fine merchandise. Terrific prices."

Lucas racked the Glocks open. "Larry talked to me about a Pug, but…"

"I'm talking Urban Warrior .223. You know how they modified the M4. The unit I got comes with an HWS site, Yankee Hill flash surpressor, and a 'Fat Boy' for sound, so you storm the Bastille you don't need to be wearing ears."

Rook put his carry gun in his shoulder rig and the other Glock in his pancake holster. "I'm not about to storm the Bastille, Franny, but I am going to Frisco."

She took off her latex gloves. "You could ship yourself something Fed Ex. People are doing that now, rather than declaring your piece in your luggage. But even though it's not in your carry-on, I hear nothing but horror stories about that. You're within your rights and their regulations and you're still on a 'watch list' forever."

"You're going to tell me you're asking me for the same kind of trouble you using Fed Ex, I'm half believing you, Francesca."

"I can't be shipping you anything decent anyway. California got one of them laws against importing anything that feeds more than ten rounds." She shook some Chiclets into her mouth. "They're just as crazy about CCW's. They bust your balls about a concealed carry permit, but you can open carry in a county with less than two hundred thousand population. Folks have a couple of twins or whatever and the population crosses that magic line, you take a pinch for exercising one of nature's most cherished rights, carrying your sidearm like Gary Cooper, Alan Ladd."

"I'm good," Rook told her. "I've got some time left on my permit from Mendocino County. Besides, from what I recall, you're legal otherwise, it's only going to cost you a couple of hundred dollar fine. Not that I wouldn't be carrying anyway, even in the type of city where the police chief's name is Heather and she has her master's degree in social work." He looked at the bill for the repair.

"What I need is for you to hook me up with a purchase out there so I don't have a waiting period. Otherwise, I got to ship."

Francesca Tanner spit out her gum and poured a couple more Chiclets into her mouth. "You'd think I'd be offering you some of this, Rook, I'm not. Not even if it gets me closer to using the box like a harmonica, which nobody can play like Larry does. You got somebody you deal with out there?"

Rook stood up on his tiptoes to stretch his bad leg. "I deal with you and Larry, Fran."

She looked at her rolodex. "No gun shops in Frisco proper. You can spread the AIDS like it's nothing, but you can't buy a gun. There's a couple of shops in South San Francisco, that's about eight miles away. The one I know is Art's. They'll be happy to rent you a couple of pounds of iron. You know the place? Has to be Glocks?"

"Or Smiths, Sigs, 9's or 45's. No Kahr's or Kimbers. And something for back-up."

"I'll call ahead, Rook. Think about that .223 I was talking about," said Mrs. Tanner. "It's sweet."

When Rook got back to the office there was another fax from Warden. They were paying expenses alright, but they were doing it on the cheap. A late flight out with a stop-over in Phoenix. On the way back, a lovely two and a half hours in Atlanta. Accommodations at the Union Square Hotel, transportation courtesy of Budget Rent-A-Car, and the meal money. Where was the Hotel Carlton and Hey Boy when you needed them?

Lucas Rook walked by Loren's Coffee Shop on the way back to his apartment. It was closed. He used to do a decent dinner trade, but that was then, this was now. Lucas tried the doorknob like his old days on the beat, remembering the day that he and his brother stopped a skel in the place. The perp had a sawed-off and a bad attitude. They zeroed him out. Now Loren was waiting to be a tycoon and Kirk had a tombstone on his forehead. Life does go on. Dragging its bloody bag of shit behind.

Rook called over to Sid Rosen that he was going out of town a couple of days so that he shouldn't get late charges on the book he hadn't read yet.

"You want me to run you out to the airport, Lucas boy?"

"You're alright, Sidney. I was going to check on Tuze, but the pencilheads I'm working for got me booked to fly out tonight. Probably save fifteen bucks or whatever. Call out there, will you?"

Rosen got up from behind his wooden desk. "Better than that, I'll make a stop tomorrow. Meanwhile, I've got to give my Fleetwood some air so I'll shoot out to the airport."

"You're too kind, Sidney," said Rook.

"Of course I am," said Rosen. "Besides, the dog likes to watch the airplanes."

They took the BQE, Sid sitting with the seat of his Caddy up close to the steering wheel to help with his night vision and Rook angled so he could stretch out his legs. The garageman's German shepherd pup was in the back on a blue blanket.

"Fish oil, Lucas boy. Good for the joints and the hair, but not cod liver, that'll kill you if you take too much."

"Fish oil, Sidney. That's good."

Rosen swung left so they could avoid the bottleneck at Northern Boulevard.

"I was talking about you, Lucas. They still wanting to do another surgery on that leg? Their wife needs another chin job, tits, whatever, they're telling you they got just the cure for what ails you." He reached his arm over the seat and patted his dog. "You go riding with your dog in the back, that's cure enough. That and fish oil, Lucas boy."

13

Rosen pulled over at the airport bus stop so that he wouldn't get hung-up in other people's hellos and goodbyes.

"This place used to be the Gala Amusement Park," he said. "The airport was named after Fiorello LaGuardia in 1964."

"I did not know that," said Lucas.

"Or that Mayor LaGuardia, the 'Little Flower,' was Jewish."

Rook got out. "Probably some of your Zionist propaganda, Sidney."

"His mother's name was Irene Coen, which makes him Jewish. You ever read some of those books I lend you, you'd find out lots of things."

"Well, then, *shalom*, Sid. *Gay gazinta hait.*"

"You 'go in good health,' too, Lucas boy."

The white airport bus stopped. It was filled with a girls lacrosse team.

"I'm telling you," the driver was saying. "There is no way that you're going to be getting on the plane with them sticks. My cousin is the fifth-ranked pool player in the country and they wouldn't let him on."

"Nobody's taking my stick," said the freckled girl in the back.

"Unless it's across their head."

"Calm down, Dales," said the coach.

"Hoot, hoot," yelled the team.

"They're going to have a big surprise from the screeners," the driver said. "Who's more than not some 10th grade drop-out colored girl with two kids at home and another on the way."

Rook looked at the driver's nameplate. "Is that right, George?"

"That is right. 'Dual use' they call it. I tried to get one of them jobs. Studied my balls off. 'Dual use' is when a seemingly harmless implement or instrument that is not a weapon can be used as a weapon. But you know the way it works. I'm a white guy, I'm driving a bus. Eighty percent of the TSA's screeners are minorities, you know."

They stopped at the next terminal. The lacrosse team got off.

"Central Terminal Building, Terminal B," George called into his microphone even though Lucas was the only passenger.

"Corkscrews are okay," said the driver. "So are knitting needles."

"Appreciate it."

"Everything we do says 'Welcome,' " said George. "That's our motto."

Rook got off. There was the usual line checking through security, traveling salesmen, vacationing families. The Arab rich boy with the Stanford cap deserved a look on general purposes, and the guy in the Yankees jacket deserved a professional going-over because he was Middle Eastern with a fresh-trimmed beard. A supervisor came over.

"Is there a problem?" he asked one of his screeners.

"I informed this gentleman that he may not bring scissors past this point."

"Am I under arrest or something?" said the passenger. "Like I told the lady, I'm …"

The passenger took a piece of paper from his pocket and began reading it as he was led to a holding area. "Ostomy scissors with pointed tips are permitted if their overall length including blades or handles is four inches or less."

"I don't know about any 'ostomy,'" said the supervisor.

A Port Authority sergeant walked up as Rook came through the screening. It was Greenburg retired out of the 4-7 in the Bronx.

"Looks like we got old home week, Rook," said Greeny.

"Right," said Lucas.

"CPR," said the sergeant.

A stocky Asian woman in a uniform came running over. "Someone need CPR?" she asked.

"No, dear," Greenburg told her. "We're fine here. It's police talk, 'Courtesy, Professional, Respect,' you know, for all people."

The detained passenger was reading from his paper louder and louder, " 'Ostomy scissors are permitted with pointed tips if their overall length including blades and handles is four inches or less when accompanied by an ostomate supply kit,' which is in my carry-on, 'containing related supplies such as collection pouches, wafers, positioning plates, tubing and adhesives.' " He started un-buttoning his shirt. "You want to see what I'm talking about, I'll show you."

"I got to get this, Rook. Meanwhile, take it light."

"You too, Greeny," said Rook.

Lucas went over and waited for his flight. A chubby family was putting on elastic bands to prevent air sickness and a hot redhead was screwing in plastic ear tubes. Where was good old Dramamine and airline scotch when you need it?

As it got close to boarding time, Rook moved over so that he could eyeball everybody getting on board. Two pairs of gaylords rushing back to Frisco where they could hold hands without wor-rying about getting beaten to death, a fat record-producer type who looked stoned. The Stanford kid and the Arab type with the fresh shave. If real security meant anything there'd be at least one air marshal on the flight. One, a blind man could make, got on and then a second, glasses, briefcase, loafers, just a hint of his carry piece.

"Retired PD," Lucas whispered.

Marshal number two ignored him and sat behind Stanford. Marshal number one was on the aisle across from clean shave. Lucas sat down and tried to work a way to keep his bad leg stretched out. The seat next to him was empty, which was a good thing, since he was getting what the insurance company paid for, which meant he was getting nothing much. The hot redhead with the ear tubes came back from the bathroom.

"I hope I won't be squishing you," she said.

" 'Squishing'?"

"You know, squashing, squeezing you. I guess that's a kid's word, 'squishing.' I teach first grade."

Lucas rearranged his posture. "I'll be glad to stay after and beat your erasers."

She held out her hand. Her grip was firm. Her skin soft. She smelled like gardenias. "I'm Teacher Arlene. I mean I'm Arlene Thorne. Although I guess with these things in my ears I look like a Vulcan or something."

"Vulcan?" said Rook.

"You know, 'Live long and prosper,'" she said. "That's from *Star Trek*."

The stewardess came into the aisle, politically correct in her lack of good looks, and made her bored presentation.

"I never could understand all that," said Arlene. "I just make sure I know where the exits are. You know, 'women and children first.' Otherwise, I just hold on to the chair and just say my prayers over and over, silently I mean. So I guess once we take off I'm not much of a conversationalist."

"Me neither," said Lucas.

The plane started its ascent. The stewardess and her male partner made two soda runs, handing out the little packages of pretzels like they were communion wafers. The trip was boring and cramped, which the gardenia smell and nice legs only partially cancelled out.

As they started the descent to Phoenix Sky Harbor International, Arlene Thorne grabbed Rook's hand, then pulled it away.

"I'm sorry," she said. "Are we supposed to get off if we're flying on?" she said. "I mean they said we can 'de-plane' if we wanted to." She started to laugh nervously. "Like *Fantasy Island*, right? De-plane, de-plane."

"It's okay, you can hold my hand anytime."

The marshals followed their Arabs out as the passengers left the plane. Lucas reached over and touched Arlene Thorne's arm and pointed to her ears. "Unless you're meeting Spock, or something."

She smiled and took the earplanes out. Rook went over to Lefty's for a couple of beers. The teacher sat in the holding area. The plane filled back up. Only one of the towelheads. The one in the Stanford cap didn't return and neither did the guy eyeballing him. Maybe another plot had been foiled, or maybe Muhammad was visiting his aunt and uncle in the Valley of the Sun.

There was one delay and then another as the plane sat on the runway in the hot, stale air. Then the captain came on the intercom to announce that they were not taking off. "Due to mechanical issues this flight is canceled. Please deplane and accept our apologies for any inconvenience. You will be entitled to a complimentary night's stay at our expense, complete with continental breakfast."

Maybe they were grounded because of something mechanical, or maybe it was the other towelhead. Either way, it was a pain in the balls.

A representative from Air Tran squired the passengers to a bus for the mile trip from PHX to the Best Western on S. 24th Street. There were about twenty of them on the bus. Rook sat next to Arlene Thorne.

"I feel safer on the ground," she said. "There's nothing we can do about it anyway. It's kind of like an adventure."

"Do you think so?" said Lucas.

"I mean not really an adventure like going down the Congo River or something like that, but it's not like getting out of New Orleans in the storm or being stuck there either." She clasped then unclasped her hands.

"I actually had relatives that died in the Galveston flood," she said. "That was in September of 1900. Over six thousand people drowned."

"I did not know that, Ms. Thorne. May I buy you a cup of coffee when we get wherever they are taking us?"

"A cup of coffee? Of course you can."

The little restaurant at the Best Western was crowded and noisy.

"How about the bar?" Lucas asked.

"As long as there's not a lot of smoke."

There were two empty seats at the bar, but a couple of wannabe junior executives in their early 30's were puffing away on cigars.

"I'd appreciate your putting them out so we can sit down," said Lucas.

The one closest held up his stogie. "There's no smoking ban here."

His buddy in the blue blazer blew a smoke ring.

Lucas walked over and put an arm around each one of them.

"I said I'd appreciate it, boys, I really would."

The blazer boy blew another smoke ring.

Rook slid his hand over a bit and pushed hard and deep on his carotid. "I'm going to hit you so hard that the little horsey on your shirt is going to shit himself," he said.

The other smoker started to say something.

"You, too," Rook told him.

"You're crazy," said Blazer.

"You're right, and I'm about to bang your heads together so that neither one of you is going to get up."

The first one put a ten on the bar. They left.

"Whatever did you tell them?" Arlene asked when they were

gone.

"Nothing much."

The bartender came over. Way too old to be wearing a ponytail.

"A glass of white wine," said Arlene Thorne.

Lucas pointed to the dirty ashtrays and ordered a Miller Lite.

"What would you have done if they hadn't put their cigars out?" Arlene asked.

"Asked them nicely to leave." He drank half his beer.

Arlene Thorne sipped her white wine.

"And if they didn't?"

"They would have."

"That sounds like an adventure," she said. "Sorry I didn't get to see it."

Rook finished his beer. "The night is young, Arlene. Maybe there'll be an encore."

"Really?" she said.

After her third glass of wine, there was.

14

The complimentary continental breakfast was stale croissants and for shit coffee, but not reason enough for Arlene Thorne to find her own way back to the airport.

Rook was scanning the sports page of *The Arizona Republic* when she walked up.

"Is everything alright?" she asked.

"The size of Barry Bonds' head is really scary," Lucas said.

She touched the collar of her blouse, then sat down.

"I mean with us. Last night."

Lucas folded his newspaper. "Sure it is. You alright?"

Arlene folded her hands. "I have never…I mean, I am. I am fine."

They sat together to wait for their flight and then on the plane like they were both strangers and old friends. When the plane touched down in San Francisco, Arlene Thorne went to get her luggage and Lucas went to the Blue Line out to the car rental.

"Goodbye," was the last thing she said. "My husband's name is James. We have two sons."

Rook picked up his rental. The tank was not full and at the $6.95 per gallon they were charging on return, he wasn't going to let it slide. He went back into the office and derailed the clerk's game of working her way through school with a siphon.

It took about twenty minutes to get to Art's Sport 'N Shoot in South San Francisco. The place was on Marina Boulevard between a liquor store and a mattress place. Cholly the Shrink would find a joke there somewhere.

Art was a furtive little guy named Poster, who was packing a chromed Colt Commander.

"What can I do you for?" he said.

"Friend of the Tanners."

Poster didn't look up. "Don't know no Tanners."

"You didn't talk to Larry or Fran, I'll just go on up the road."

"Don't want you to do that." This time he offered what he considered eye contact. "I do recall I spoke to them. You buying or selling, friend?"

"You talked to her."

"Right," Poster said. He leaned forward. "Got a beautiful Llama .45 for you. Beautiful."

"Glocks, 21 and a 30. Extra magazine. No reloads."

The gun man brought up the 21. " 'Glock and Load' it is. I'll throw in a box of Winchester SXT's if you pay cash." Then he offered up a Kimber for the second piece as if Rook wouldn't notice.

Lucas leaned forward. "You have the other Glock or not?"

Poster stepped back. "Do I detect a note of hostility? I was only trying to accommodate you. I do have a Glock 19, cherry condition, but I did not feel you wanted to be bothered with the ammo is all. You're wanting a compact .45, I got a beautiful Sig 245, blued. Pre-owned with a factory warranty."

"We can do business if you're not going to pull any shit when I come back."

Poster got the Sig .45 from the gun safe. "You pay cash now. I pay you with a check when you come back if there's no damage or you don't put no crimes on it, which is why I pay you at the back end with a check."

Rook examined the weapons and showed the cash. "The ammo's on the house," he said as Poster wrote it up.

"Right, right, I almost forgot. You need a case, locks, cleaning kits, I'll make you a deal."

"I bet you will," said Lucas. And he walked out.

The ride up Route 101 to San Francisco went quick except for the junction at 80. If you're going to San Francisco put flowers in your hair or a pair of .45's under the seat. The home of Palladin, the earthquake, Alcatraz. Now Judy Garland and Liza Minnelli. The last time he was there was to meet with Joe Azzioli and do that job out in the counties at a hefty rate.

This time it was the Union Square Hotel between the Quiznos' and the Jack in the Box, courtesy of the big spenders at the insurance company. At least there was Max's up the block where he could get some decent New York food. And it was walking distance to the last known address that Dwight Graves had given up for a handshake with Ulysses Grant in it.

Maybe it was worth it, maybe it wasn't. You're looking for a *moolie* with the name D'Angelo Anthony who works as a cook in Frisco, you don't have to be a genius. Then again, it doesn't pay to down the detective who ran the case because he got his hand out and you're going to be able to expense it anyway.

Lucas checked into the hotel. The desk was run by a surfer type whose face went blank when asked if there was a law enforcement discount. The manager came over.

"I'm Harvey Green. How may I be of service?"

Rook tinned him and the manager asked him to come into his office, a small room to the right with too many prints of the Golden Gate Bridge.

"Is there a problem, officer?"

Lucas took a glance at the nameplate on his desk.

"It's 'detective,' Mr. Green. And no, there's not. I was inquiring whether or not you give a law enforcement discount."

Harvey Green sat down and scrolled through his computer.

"You've been pre-paid at a corporate discount, which actually is somewhat greater than the serviceman and LE discount."

"That says something," Lucas told him.

"I guess it does, although I'm not sure what. I will, however, be pleased to offer you a discount on your parking and two free in-room movies."

"Appreciate it," Rook said and went up into his room.

The view was the building next door and the tub was too small for him to stretch out. Lucas left his bag on the bed and walked over to Union Square with his Glock .45 and Sig back-up.

Rook walked the area first. You always did that, whether it was walking the beat when Kirk and him were first on the job or working one of those cases that was a mind fuck even if you're on the job for twenty years.

Now he wasn't putting down the bad guys or shaking doors, but checking out the windows of Armani, Dior and Jack Bell. Then past the benches on Geary Street and through the palm trees, Admiral Dewey's statue with the bronze woman on top that made it through the earthquake.

At the far end of the square was an Italian joint, Sal Patti's. The place didn't open for an hour anyway. Rook went over to Chinatown to see the shop owners and tourists watching each other. Maybe get something for his bad leg that was acting up.

Through the Grant Avenue entrance, "All Under Heaven is for the Good of the People" was the motto on the gate. Sure, just like the crap marked up a thousand percent in the souvenir shops and the McDonald's on the first floor of the Sing Chong Building.

He found a Chinese medicine shop on Tong Yun Gai Street.

"I'm looking for something for my leg, arthritis or whatever," he told the sales clerk.

"*Shuguan wenjing chongji* or *shugan quing luo*?" she asked.

"How about some Advils, then," Rook said.

She made a little bow and the owner came out from the back. Half Chinese, half American.

"She was asking whether it was for the yang or for the yin."

"It's for the leg."

"Maybe it's for the deer penis," he said with a little laugh. "You know, Steven Segal in *Glimmer Man* before he turned into Refrigerator Perry. I'm Marvin Lederer." He offered his hand.

"Right, Marvin. Just looking for something for an old injury."

"Maybe yes, maybe no. Your leg pain is just as likely to be from an imbalance in your liver."

Lucas turned to go. "Appreciate it, Doc. I'll stick with the Advils."

"Try arnica," Lederer told him. "Any health food store or decent drug store carries it. It's a gel. Works for me."

Rook walked by the old St. Mary's Church at California and Geary. "Son, Observe the Time and Fly from Evil" read the biblical quote on the clock. One out of two wasn't bad. He checked his watch and went back to Sal's.

It was a coffee and pastry joint. Espresso, cappuccino at $5.25 a pop and pastries absolutely not done on the premises. No way the place was anything but a laundry. There was a swarthy man working the tables and another behind the register. He was big, 250 or more, with a monogrammed shirt and gold cuff links.

"I'm looking for D'Angelo Anthony," Rook said.

"And you're thinking I'm going to tell you that I don't talk to cops. Well, you're wrong there. Anthony's a thief, had his fingers in the till. So you're looking for him, he's working at some hippy dippy restaurant down at the Haight where it's easier for him to feed his reefer habit."

Lucas left a five for the coffee he didn't have. "So much for *omerta*," he said on the way out.

"I heard that," said the big man.

15

Anthony D'Angelo's father worked the late shift fixing cable cars after his wife died so he could look after his son as much as he could. Fortunately for Anthony, there was Uncle Severrio and his wife, Beatrice, who lived five houses down the block in the close-knit Sicilian community.

Uncle Sevvy used to be a fisherman and loved the Yanks. Aunt Bea cooked sausage in her iron pan and baked bread that smelled like cake. Anthony slept on their pull-out couch that almost filled their warm front room, and Uncle Sevvy told good night stories of Frankie the Crow and in the morning they walked Anthony home with his pajamas on underneath his coat.

Frankie the Crow was Frank Crosetti, Sevvy's cousin, who spent forty years with the Yankees as a player and a coach. Cousin Frank had so many World Series rings, Uncle Sevvy used to say, that he had one for every finger and every toe and some left over if he wanted to change them around a bit. When Aunt Bea was stirring something good in the pot with her favorite wooden spoon, Uncle Sevvy used to tell stories about Cousin Frank sliding into second with his spikes up high and how he led the league in '38 in stolen bases and putouts and assists. How the Crow was the master of the hidden ball trick that sent many a member of the enemy to the dugout in humiliation. There were stories of Tony Lazzeri, "Poosh 'em up" Tony, who came out of the mist around the fishermen's neighborhood to become one of the "Murderers Row" with the Babe and Lou Gehrig, the Iron Horse. There was Dario Ludigiani, who hit .395 for the hated Oakland Oaks before getting called up to play for the Philly A's. And then there was the DiMaggio boys, three brothers, who were like gods, Vince and Dom and Joe D, the very best of all.

When Uncle Sevvy spoke about Joe DiMaggio, he poured a glass of his home made wine and just a taste for Anthony. The Yankee Clipper, the Last American Hero, who hit in 62 straight games for the San Francisco Seals before the New York Yankees bought out his contract even after he broke his knee and the Seals would only agree if the Yanks let him stay another year.

Joe DiMaggio who was one of them because his father was a fisherman, was an All Star thirteen times and MVP three. He hit .381 one year and another socked 46 out of the park and knocked in 167 runs. A war hero too. He won all those World Series and set the record that no one will ever break, hitting safe in 56 Major League games. And he married Marilyn Monroe.

Anthony D'Angelo wasn't Joe D or Frankie the Crow. After he had learned a trade, working from busboy to the kitchen at Castagnola's, Anthony D'Angelo said goodbye to Aunt Bea and Uncle Sevvy, his father gone and buried like his mother, and left behind the fog and mist to find his life.

There was a close-knit Sicilian community in New York in the shadow of Yankee Stadium, where Frank the Crow played short-stop and where Joe D made running in the outfield a thing of art. The Bronx neighborhood known as Belmont had lots of restaurants for Anthony. He found an upstairs apartment behind Our Lady of Mt. Carmel, and with his letter from Castagnola's and a little help from the Bronx Italian American Committee, got a job at Briglia's, which was famous for their clams, the mussels and the calamar.

Carol Briglia was as light as the rest of her Sicilian family was dark, 'the lily,' her older brother, Carmine, called her. She was in her third year at Fordham when they first met, her coming through the kitchen with her bag of books. She was blonde and white like Marilyn Monroe, but Anthony was straining pasta, not hitting home-runs.

"She's my sister," Carmine said when she was gone.

"Oh," said Anthony D'Angelo. "I see."

"That's all you do," the big brother said.

But Carol Briglia had other ideas if only to make him squirm. Anthony misunderstood when she took him to sign up for a course at Fordham not-for-credit. It was called "Success in the Food Industry Trade," so it was not all a loss.

Anthony kept his apartment on the second floor behind Our Lady of Mt. Carmel's, but said goodbye to Briglia's when Carol got engaged to a doctor who worked at St. Barnabus, and he took a position in a decent restaurant on Mulberry Street, walking the fifteen minutes to the D train and then down to Little Italy.

He first saw Helen Maguire at the Feast of San Gennaro the following September. She was blocking the parade at Grand and Mott, having taken a wrong turn in her brother's car, as out of place with her Irish looks as was her car in the festival's procession. Helen Maguire, with her green eyes and red hair, was scared, then angry, then both as she got out and left the keys. Anthony D'Angelo came over with his arms filled with extra bread from Villotti's up the street and shook his head and laughed as much at the spectacle itself as to calm the redhead down and the Sicilian revelers, who were yelling at her to move the car.

Anthony put the loaves on the car roof and then got into the driver's side.

"Go, Tony," yelled someone from the crowd.

"Take the *medigan* back where she belongs," said someone else.

And he might have, had he not had work to do, and she knew that his Sicilian looks would get a bad reception if he drove her to Hell's Kitchen where she was from. Helen Maguire handed him her phone number when he pulled her car over on Canal Street. "I'd like to buy you a beer, or a cup of coffee to say thanks," she said.

He waited two days to call the Irish girl so he wouldn't seem overanxious and then another day because he was.

"It's Tony," he said. "From the other day. I wasn't sure if you were serious or not, but I would like to buy you a cup of coffee."

"Sure," she said. "We could meet after work in the library."

"The one with the lions out front?"

"No," she told him. "It's on the Avenue, Tenth. Inside in the geography section."

Anthony and Helen met twice in the library before she let them meet for coffee in the Village.

"I could pick you up at work," he said.

"I don't think so," she said as she sipped her tea.

"Why's that?"

"Because I work at the Market Diner is why."

"I don't get it, Helen. I mean, I'm not from here."

She held the cup to warm her hands. "That's just it, I mean."

"You mean you've got red hair and freckles and I'm a 'guinea'?"

Helen leaned forward. "I don't mean that, or even think that, but my brother would, and the people around him."

"Which is why I couldn't come to your work?"

"My brother's very protective. And the diner is where West Siders hang out. Jimmy Coogan," she whispered.

He shrugged his shoulders.

"The West Siders, the Westies." She leaned forward. "The Irish mob."

He finished his coffee. "My people know a little bit about such things, Helen Maguire. Now am I going to get to take you to the movies or not?"

"Your eyes got all smoldery for a minute there, Anthony

D'Angelo. Is that some Italian thing?"

"I guess it is," he said.

They went to the movies twice and then walked in Central Park before sitting close on the ride downtown. They kissed on the subway platform and then couldn't keep away from each other until they went away to Wildwood, where they made love for the first time as if they were meant for each other.

But one of the West Side Boys saw them together at the Snow White hot dog stand on the boardwalk. This got back to Helen's brother, Reds, and to one of Jimmy Coogan's men. Reds was fuming that his sister was keeping time with a wop and there was talk that Coogan himself found it a personal insult that Helen, who was like a daughter to him for pouring his coffee at the Market Diner, was seeing a dago.

Reds and his roomie, Big Eddie Kelly, paid Anthony D'Angelo a visit while he was walking from the D train to work.

"You putting shame on my sister?" said Reds, showing the butt of his .38.

"Do I know you?" said Anthony.

"You don't want to," said Eddie.

Reds moved in. "Listen, shit-for-brains. I hear you're around Helen anymore, there won't be enough of you to make meatballs out of."

"Without a doubt. Without a doubt," said Kelly. And he spit before they moved on.

Reds Maguire had it out with his sister too, about how she was betraying her people and insulting people you don't insult. But he should have known that talking to Helen wouldn't work. Like he should have guessed his sister had Anthony meet her in front of the Jukebox Café at 45th and 10th. This got Tony a beating and his place in the Bronx got trashed. And Anthony and Helen, they were on their way to being some kind of Hell's Kitchen Romeo and Juliet.

16

Rook's ride from his hotel took him through Japan Town. Only in San Fran. Japan Town, China Town. How about Fag Town? Bleeding Heart Liberal Town?

He found Tony D'Angelo making pizza in a tourist trap in Haight Ashbury between Dreams of Kathmandu and the Live Healthy Nutrition Center. Not D'Angelo Anthony, the black man, but Anthony D'Angelo, the Sicilian. The Italians called the *siggis* Africans. So in addition to being a douche bag, Dwight Graves was a comedian.

D'Angelo was working the oven and the cash register and had the wasted eyes, wasted life look. Not a good combination. A flash of a gold shield got those eyes to widen.

"We can talk here or take a ride," Rook said.

"I'm working." Anthony turned to check a pie with his long wood paddle.

"Bet you're holding too. Just a little talk, Tony. We can do this nice and nonchalant or we can take a look at why your pupils are all pinned."

Two middle-aged customers walked in on platform shoes.

"Slice and a diet Sprite," said the man in the Hendrix shirt.

"I brought my water in," said his wife.

"You want me to take a look at Sonny and Cher here too, Tony?" said Lucas.

"Give me a minute," he said. He rang them up. "My cashier comes in twenty minutes or so. We can sit down in the back. I'll buy you a Coke."

Rook sat in a booth close enough to the front door and the back so Anthony wasn't going anywhere. In about twenty minutes the waitress came in. A pimply girl trying to make herself look pretty with purple hair and a cigarette.

"Told you before, Ronnie. No smoking here," said D'Angelo.

She did a little salute. "Yessir, boss, I forgot, sir." She chinked her cigarette and put it in her shirt pocket.

"Nice," Anthony told her. Rook followed him to a table in the back. Then Anthony got up to wipe it off and fill two soda cups.

"The only coke I do, detective. Honest."

Lucas sat down. "Whatever you say. You used to work over at Union Square."

"They ran me out. Said I was taking from them, but I never would. I know better."

"You're a fine citizen."

"More who they are. Everybody works in the restaurant business handles cash, they pinch some. But not if you work for *them*. You know who I mean."

"This place different, Tony?"

He sipped his soda. "Some hook-nosed Jew and his big tit wife from White Plains. They own a couple of joints on the street, Pipe Dreams, The Purple Nurple and what not." He took a Marlboro Light from the box in his pocket.

Rook knocked it out of his hand. "Against the law to smoke in here, Anthony."

The pizza man slid his chair back and folded his arms.

"You been back East or the West Side Boys got you exiled?" Lucas asked.

"I go and come where I want."

"Right, and your own people won't have you here either."

D'Angelo looked around the room. "You want something? I got to get back to work."

"Sure, sure." Rook picked the cigarette off the table and handed it back to him. "A cup of bad coffee, a couple of more questions, I'm out of here."

Anthony waved to the girl with the purple hair.

"A cup of coffee for my friend here, Ronnie."

Rook leaned in and put his hand on D'Angelo's arm. He was thin, but strong.

"You're a smart guy," Lucas said. "Now give me the right answers and I'm out of here, bad coffee and all."

D'Angelo lit his smoke. "Sure, sure," he said. "Let's get this over with. I'm not going to shit you."

"You got that right," Lucas said. "Now just tell me, you kiss Helen goodbye before or after you did what you had to do?"

Anthony paled. "Helen?"

"Right, Romeo."

"Is she alright?"

Rook leaned in. "She's fine if you don't count her broken neck and choking on her own vomit. Then again, there was all that blood."

Anthony D'Angelo started to get up, then sat back down. "Helen," he said.

The coffee came. Anthony waved the girl away.

"You want me to tell you about it, Tony? You're here, you're there. You're together, you're apart. She's dead, you're alive. I know about the kid."

"We were…Do we have to do this now? I don't feel so good."

"Depends on what you got to say, Anthony. Maybe you got your whole lifetime to talk about it. You can wave to all the tourists when they open Alcatraz for you. You're a lowlife, penny ante thief, kills his girlfriend when she decides her brother was right, she got to stick to her own kind. And leaves his kid in the street."

Anthony shook his head.

"It wasn't like that. I loved her. She loved me." He shook his head again. "It wasn't like that."

Rook looked at his watch. "I'm going to give you five minutes. You give me everything you got, I help you make this easier on you. The homicide's not my case. Let them back in New York worry about it. I just got some loose ends to tie up."

"I don't…"

"Four minutes, thirty seconds."

Anthony D'Angelo dropped his cigarette into the Styrofoam cup. "I met her, we fell in love. Her brother and some of his tough guy friends didn't like that. The micks and the Italians were trying to get their mob business together then. Jimmy Coogan. Paul Castellano. Some of them tried to make me and Helen a political thing. Then the don, Castellano, he gets whacked outside of Sparks. Him and his bodyguard, John Bilotti." He lit another smoke.

"Tom. Tommy Bilotti," said Lucas.

"Right, right. Then John Gotti's the don and he knows me from coming into the restaurant, and Mickey Featherstone, a big Irish mob guy, goes over to the Feds. They all go down, the Westies' Jimmy Coogan, Billy Bokun, Ritter, even Coogan's wife. And Tommy Maguire's wife. They get pinched. Half of them's singing like canaries. Rudy Giuliani is a hero."

Rook looked at his watch again. "Helen?" he said.

"John Gotti says I'm alright, nobody bothers us."

"You're running out of time, lover boy."

"She got pregnant. She had the baby." Anthony looked away then back again. "A son, I didn't even see him. She gave him away to Catholic Services. Some place upstate. She went, she came back."

"And you?"

"I tried for us to stay together. But she never forgave me. Somehow she blamed me for it all. She started to drink. They do that, the Irish. She drank and drank. She became a drunk."

"You prefer to smoke it, Tony boy?"

"Helen never forgave me."

"For knocking her up, Tony. Not marrying her. What? You got three more minutes."

"Then she wanted to find the boy. Said she couldn't sleep. John Gotti took care of it. He found him. His name was Anthony too. Can you believe that, just like me. Can you believe that? And after all that he's taken in by Italians. Then he died." Anthony D'Angelo put his head down. "Just a kid and he died. My son and I never even saw him. Seven years old. I tried to be with her, but Helen, she wouldn't have it. Then the Feds take Gotti down and she's a lush and her brother's blaming me for that too. So off I go. Back home, here. You know, 'Where you gone, Joe DiMaggio?'" He started to cry.

"You get back there, Anthony. You miss her. You can't forgive her throwing you out. You get back to the Big Apple. She's loaded. You two get at it with her Irish temper. She pushes you, you push her back. Helen takes a header. That's all she wrote."

Anthony took a deep breath. "Once a year. On the anniversary of his death, I would go to the grave. Helen would be there. She wouldn't talk to me, but we were both, I mean the three of us were there."

"And then you two got at it."

"She never spoke to me. Never a word."

"When your boy die, Anthony?"

"Easter," said the pizza man. "Easter Sunday, can you believe that?"

"Sure," said Lucas Rook. "I believe that." He got up. "Now you have a nice day, Anthony, you really do. And this doesn't check out, you'll have more than a couple of washed-up West Side boys to worry about."

Rook drove back to Tourist Town. Max's was jammed. The pastrami sandwich up the street was an insult. But soon enough he would get back to New York. Eat something decent, check out the pizza man's story. Think of how he was going to play that this new beneficiary had been in the ground for years. And maybe have a little chat with the detective who thought he was Bill Cosby.

The flight back wasn't bad except for the snoring man in the cowboy hat. A couple of doll house bottles of scotch to pass the time. Lucas stretched his leg as best he could in the cheap seats the insurance company had sprung for. He remembered the days when the West Side Gang were badasses. You're thinking about the Paddy-boys, you're doing research on those bad actors.

Rook toasted himself and made a mental note to bill the time.

17

Eddie Kelly snubbed his Lucky out in the yolk of his egg. "We don't hardly exist no more," he said as he pushed his plate away.

"I wished you would've told me before you beat me them last two games of shuffleboard up McGinty's last night," Reds Maguire said. "I don't owe you no beers since we don't exist no more."

Eddie got up and took his plate to the sink. "You know what I mean. Us, the old neighborhood, Richie Ryan, Coonan's crew, whatever."

Reds squirted on the Palmolive. "We'd been with them anymore than we was, we'd be with them now, in the joint, in the river, dead. Besides, half of them went rat to the Feds, the other half were psycho, Richie shoving his .38 up Tommy Hess's ass."

"Right, right. And I'm not sorry for what I done," Kelly said. "While I'm away, they teach me how to cut meat, so when I come back I know you don't take them apart, the lungs, whatever inflate and what you got is a floater or whatever."

Reds fished a Kool from his shirt pocket. "You just reminded me, get some of them black plastic garbage bags, when you go up to the check cash."

"You're kidding me, right? You talking about taking somebody apart?"

"I'm kidding you, Eddie. But before you go, fold up the roll away."

"We expecting company?" asked Kelly.

"Right, right. Ed Sullivan's coming over to hear you sing. And you got any pretzels or whatever in there, I'd appreciate your getting them out for me so we don't have no more rodents coming around."

Maguire wiped the table down into the cup of his hand and brushed it into the sink. "So I was half a wiseguy working the docks when there was any and you was damn good at your trade before the butcher's union let them bring all that boxed meat. That was then, this is now."

Eddie Kelly left. Reds finished cleaning up their little breakfast. Eddie was right. It wasn't the same. Hadn't been the same, really, since the elevated train came down and most of the Irish moved to the suburbs, letting in the blacks and the Puerto Ricans, and the queers. You knew it was over when the Garden moved from 50th. At least all the politicians and the developers from Connecticut or wherever got to choke on it that the Olympics and the stadiums fell through. All of them rich guys had it up their ass talking about a "New Manhattan."

Reds went over to the calendar he had gotten from Clinton Glass. Tomorrow he had the last treatment on the warts on his foot. And he was supposed to make another payment on Helen's funeral bill.

He went into the other room and shook out the sheet on the fold-away. Some things Eddie did and some things he didn't. He didn't always remember to do what he said he'd do, like close up the sofa bed like he said, and he never said anything when he left. "You'll know I'm gone when you don't hear me say nothing," was Eddie's motto. But if you needed somebody to pay their share of the rent or watch your back, Eddie was the guy.

"Hello," said somebody at the apartment door.

"We don't want any," Reds told them.

"It's your neighbor from the CCO."

"I don't have any." Reds lit a menthol.

"The Clinton Community Organization, to get your input on…"

Reds Maguire went to the door. "Look, missy or mister or whatever, I don't have any. I don't want any. And you don't want me talking about no inputs, so have a nice day."

Do-gooders, meddlers, liars. Just like the asshole mother fuckers at the Local. You put in your time, you pay your dues, get your hours in, then you don't have a job because they made them all go away to line their own pockets.

Reds started up the vac again, then shut it down to go out and have another smoke on the fire escape. He hoped Eddie didn't go to the OTB where he could forget where he was. Then he'd have to go up on the Avenue where a carton of Kools cost a million dollars and you couldn't even find the shorties without the fillers.

It used to be good all the time out on the fire escape. Now you had yuppies and the girlie boys out there and talking about their ferns and their "community" gardens across the street. So Reds and Eddie started giving everybody the evil eye so if they came out of their apartment to get a smoke or have a cold one, they got left alone.

Reds lit up his unfiltered Kool and leaned back against the bricks. It was bad fucked up that Helen had fallen down and broke her neck. He was the only one of them left now. It was just him and Eddie Kelly now, which wasn't so bad, if once a year or whatever, he remembered to close the fold-away.

Reds was putting the trash out when he saw Lucas Rook park across the street and start over.

"You got a check for me? Otherwise, I'm not home."

"I need to talk to you," said Lucas.

Maguire finished his smoke and flicked the butt. "We're done with that."

"Don't want to chat you up in the street," Rook said. "In fact, I don't want to have a little chit-chat at all. Except I got my job to do before we close this out and you get paid. I won't take but ten minutes. It'll help me move the papers along."

"Not in my place you don't. You swing on up the Avenue, pick up a couple of packs of Kool unfiltered, maybe we have our little talk, but not in here."

Lucas turned and walked back across the street. "I'll grab us a bench. We can hold hands."

He went around the block and came back with two cups of coffee and two packs of smokes.

"You think you can buy me off for a cup of coffee?"

"Not unless it's one of them $8-a-cup Starbucks with the whipped cream swirls," said Lucas.

Maguire put the packs of cigarettes in his shirt pockets then opened his coffee. "You didn't come by to be my friend. We talking, it's only about me getting my check."

"Not about your happy days at the Elmira Reformatory, Reds? Or your roomie made it to the big time? Must be just peachy you're rooming with somebody that'd pat your face with a shovel you look the wrong way."

Reds lit up one of his menthols. "Eddie told me he knows you."

Lucas took a sip of coffee. "Probably, Eddie's brain damaged from biting the pillow for his cellmate up in Attica. But enough of the good old days. You want the insurance money, I want to ask you about the boyfriend."

"The who?"

"Anthony D'Angelo, Reds."

"Wop mother fucker."

"Tell me how you really feel," Lucas said.

Maguire took a long drag on his Kool. "Up to me, he'd be a dead man."

Lucas shifted his weapon in case the next push at Maguire would take him too far.

"No way to talk about a family member, Uncle. Anthony giving you a wop nephew and all."

"What the fuck you saying?" Maguire flicked his cigarette at Rook.

"Oh, my," Lucas said. "You about to see the fifty grand go up in smoke?"

Reds Maguire started at Rook then stopped. "Fuck you," he said. "Fuck you."

"You want to hear what I got to say or what? Otherwise, I'm out of here."

Eddie Kelly came up. "What the fuck?" he said.

"He was just leaving," said Reds.

"Right, right. That's what he does." He turned to Rook. "You tried to roust me for nothing. You had your hand out. I kicked your ass. You hit like a girl."

Rook brought his blackjack out, fast and hard. Once to Eddie's collarbone and then above his ear. Kelly went down.

"When your boyfriend wakes up, Maguire, you tell him he wants more, I got it."

Reds started at him.

Lucas showed his .45. "I don't shoot like a girl either. You don't keep Eddie on a leash or you even look at me sideways, you can forget about the insurance money, not to mention getting up in the morning."

Eddie Kelly groaned and tried to stand. "What happened?" he said.

"I'll tell you about it," said Reds.

Rook took one of his business cards with the chess piece on it and stuck it in Maguire's shirt pocket. "Now you two girls have a nice day," he said.

He waited across the street for the pus bags to go back inside. Eddie Kelly with the knot on his head and most likely a broken clavicle and Reds Maguire, half into being a tough guy and half into the insurance check that would keep him in Four Roses and smokes forever. A couple of mothers brought their strollers over to the Clinton Gardens and a black lady wheeling blond twins went by.

Lucas drove over to Greenpoint Avenue and back, thinking about another pass at the washed-up Westies. He saw the two of them walking west on 50th Street. Kelly didn't look so good, trying to light his cigarette left-handed. Lucas slowed down and opened his window. "You two Whyos going for a little stroll?"

"You snuck me, asshole. And you wish you hadn't," said Kelly.

"You got a big mouth, Rook," said Maguire.

"And when I get back, I'm going to shut it for you," said Kelly.

"You didn't do so good with two hands, Eddie," Rook told him. "You going up to St. Luke's you ask them to check your head, doesn't seem your brain's working too good."

Eddie gave Lucas the finger, but Reds threw him an OK sign behind his back. Rook turned the corner and drove over to his office. For what they got for parking even at his end of 5th Avenue, it paid to drive downtown to Sid's and cab it back up unless a parking space opened up. A UPS truck was unloading three spots down from 166. The driver was a blonde woman, almost six foot and built like a weight lifter.

"You coming out?" Rook asked her.

"Soon as I drop off this load."

"I'll swing around."

"You do that, honey. Knock yourself out," she told him.

By the time he got around again, the spot was taken by a Con-Ed truck. Lucas drove on down to Rosen's garage. Sid was behind his wooden desk cleaning a chromed carburetor.

"You ever use those specs of yours except to keep the top of your head warm, Sidney?"

"These are my reading glasses. I got my reading glasses, which I'm not doing, and in my desk here I got my drinking glasses."

Rook sat down. "You buying?"

Rosen took the bottle and the two glasses from his bottom

drawer. "You got that you-want-to-break-somebody's-head look. More than usual." He poured them each a drink.

Lucas finished his Wild Turkey and tapped his glass for another.

Sid poured a refill. "*L'chaim*," he said.

"Times two," said Rook.

"Who's the lucky girl?" asked Rosen.

Rook sipped his drink. "Couple of Westie leftovers I'm saying hello to. Working one on an insurance job."

Sid picked up the carburetor again. "Those were the days, the Coonan-Spillane wars and Jimmy C trying to hook up with the Italian boys." He wiped his hands. "I could half way figure Mickey Featherstone going stoolie, the Feds can do that. Besides, he was mostly a bag of nuts anyway."

Sid finished his drink and offered another, but Rook waved him off. "The other thing I can't figure out though."

"You got that look in your eye, Mr. Rosen. I'll bite."

"The Spillane thing. I mean, Mickey got all them best sellers and what not."

"I know there're two Mickey Spillanes, Sid, one the writer, who died a couple of months ago, one the skel."

"True, true, but what you did not know is that Mickey Spillane, the writer, was named Frank Morrison Spillane, and he went from Brooklyn to college in Kansas. Was a captain in the Air Force."

Lucas got up. "I did not know that, Sidney. I surely didn't. Especially the Kansas part. Maybe he met Dorothy there or whatever."

"Now there's a thought, Lucas boy. I like that. I surely do."

Rook went over to Joe Oren's for a cup of coffee and a piece of pie. Joe and Jeanie were sitting at the counter. Jeanie had on her poker-playing hat.

"Family meeting?" Rook asked.

"You're family, Uncle Lucas," said Jeanie.

Oren went around to the back of the counter and poured an-

other cup of coffee. "She wants to transfer to the Fashion Institute. I said you're almost done at NYU, stick it out, then we can talk
about it."

Jeanie stirred her coffee with her finger. "I cannot stand NYU.
They are liars and phonies pretending to be all egalitarian and for
women and diversity, but they're nothing but a bunch of crypto
fascists."

"That computer thing?" Rook asked.

"Because of you and Daddy it went away. Otherwise, they'd
have taken me down the basement like Anastasia."

"She means the Russian princess, not Murder Incorporated,"
her father said.

"Besides, I'm definitely committed to a career in cosmetics
and fragrances. That's big business, you know."

"I'm sure it is, Jeanie, but like your dad said…"

Sam came in. "You starting into playing without me. Usually
you wait for a gentleman to take his seat before you deals them
out."

The cook took the seat next to Lucas.

"I do not want to go back to that fraudulent school," said
Jeanie. "I do want to work in the fashion industry."

Joe Oren took a lemon meringue pie from the plexiglass case.

"Pie doesn't cure everything," Jeanie said.

"Goes a long way," said the cook.

"You're almost done," said Joe. "Then you can take a masters
at the Fashion Institute."

"Or even study with Pierantozzi," said Lucas.

"How do you know about him? He's so famous in the fashion
industry."

"My neighbor, Gracey, knows him. Maybe in the meantime,
you can go out with her on one of her shoots."

"Right," said Joe. "While you're finishing over at NYU."

She got up and did the runway walk. "I'd like to do that, if
Daddy says okay. Maybe that will get me through. Meanwhile, let's

have some dessert."

Grace was on Rook's answering machine when he got back to his apartment. "I'm busy," she said. "Morphing."

Rook called her back. "I won't ask you're morphing into what," he said.

"Okie dokie," she said. "Thanks for the invitation. I'll be over when I'm ready."

Babysitting with whichever Gracey came from across the hall was enough to make you yearn for the good old days of sitting in a cold stakeout car and pissing in a jar. Lucas ran through the channels. *Man on Fire* to the rescue. He poured himself a cold one and watched Denzel do his avenging angel shit for the dozenth time.

The shootouts, not to mention the bad guy getting blown up by the bomb in his ass, were enough to give any man an appetite, but the cupboard was bare.

Lucas called around the corner for the Cambodians acting like they were Pakistanis selling Chinese. The delivery boy was Mexican. Rook was half way through his pork lo mein when he saw somebody climb over the low wall between Grace's patio and his.

It was Gracey wrapped in a purple dressing gown on which she had painted yellow flowers. When she came to the sliding glass door she opened her wrap. Her angular white body was covered with purple irises.

"I drew them myself," she said. "From the memory of somebody else's words." Grace Savoy opened and closed her robe, like the wings of a fluttering bird. "It is a celebration and memorial for the fragile, murdered ones."

18

Breakfast meant two cups of coffee. Doc Fenton leaves you a message, "Your LDL is not good," maybe it's goodbye to the salami and eggs, but no way you start the day with oatmeal and flaxseed or whatever. The next thing you know it's Postum and prunes.

No appointments meant he could wear what he wanted, which meant the black sweats. There was a suit and tie in the office if maybe he had to look like the part in an emergency. Eleven o'clock became an emergency because that's when Everett Warden called to say he'd be by.

Lucas had enough time to change into his suit, get his paperwork together on the fall down job, and even straighten up the office a bit. Too bad there wasn't enough to hire an interior decorator. He was half way through cleaning up the mess that was his desk when Manny knocked on his door.

"I got good news and bad news," the super said. "The good news is the elevators will be down for an hour, the bad news is I'll be away for a while on that thing."

"You need anything, look after your kid, whatever?"

"Appreciate that. He's a good boy. It hurts me because of

him." He turned away. "I'll see you when I'm done," said Manny and he walked away.

Warden called again. "I'm sorry," he said. "But we have to re-schedule our meeting, or rather cancel, because we can have the discussion now. It was for the purpose of telling you that I need your services for the next two evenings, three hours each. Two-fifty an evening, no reports or preparation. Right here in the city."

"I'll move some things around."

"I appreciate that, Rook. Saturday is black tie."

"What's up?"

"The Pennsylvania Society. I have some meetings. Our integrity officer's wife's having a C-section. What I need you to do is accompany me and look like you're listening to every word they say."

"I do that," said Lucas.

"I know you do," said Warden. "And you can call me Dick, except at the meetings. Also, if you can't fill the time you set aside for today's meeting, let me know, we'll work that out. Time is money on both sides."

"What time do you need me, Dick?"

"First meeting is Friday at eight. Dinner at the Bull and Bear, right in the Waldorf."

"That's stretching out my day, Mr. Warden, you're running to almost midnight."

"If you're looking for some kind of kicker on the rates, I've got no wiggle room here."

The "Dick" stuff keeps right on going. So does the good news, bad news. Good news you don't have to dust or run out and buy doilies for the office. The bad news is the tux thing. You got to go rent one, not to mention you're going to be surrounded by the out-of-town penguins taking over the city for the weekend. They call it "Pennsylvania" Society, they should keep all their big cocktail parties and public officials mauling their administrative aides down in Philly, Pittsburgh even.

Braits was four blocks up Fifth Avenue on the third floor. Sarkissian had sent him there once before because he didn't do tuxes. Lucas was thinking about how the old man had shot his piece of crap kid and then himself when the salesman walked over.

"My name is Scott. Do you have an account with us?"

"I don't. I need the penguin outfit, just the suit, size 50."

"You have the accessories? They're included in our Gotham Special."

"Your Gotham Special's not special enough."

"You get a sharp ensemble for $199.99, sir," said Scott.

"For that, I'm wearing a white shirt and tie as my 'ensemble,' whatever that is."

"You are joking," said the salesman.

"Do I look like I joke?"

"No, you don't. We do have something for somewhat less, but I'm afraid it's last year's style."

"Oh, that's a pity. How much less are we talking?"

The salesman went over to his manager and then came back. "$129.99, but I'm afraid a 50 will be a little big."

"That will be just fine," Rook said.

"You can pick it up by five on Friday. It's due back Monday at five. We require a fifty-dollar deposit."

Lucas gave him the cash. "Didn't I see you in a commercial or something?"

"You could have." He leaned in. "I'll not charge you for the cummerbund set."

Lucas went back to the office. The elevators were down early. Likely as not, Manny's way of saying fuck you before he went to the can. There was about fifteen minutes before the chicken salad crowd hit the deli. You have a tongue on rye, diet cream soda, even Brad Fenton's not having a fit. Sol's was out of tongue, but then again, they had been out of Sol for ten years, and Soo Il Kuk, who ran the place, didn't appreciate the imperative of keeping the deli stocked with deli.

"I got lean corned beef, real lean. Or turkey pastrami," he said. "I'm you I'd go for the corned beef."

"You're me, Soo, you'd be making a tongue sandwich."

"So?"

"So, Soo, turkey pastrami isn't pastrami."

"So sue me, so sue Soo. You get it?"

Lucas sat down to stretch his bad leg. "Your command of the language is wonderful. A regular 'ensemble.' "

"Corned beef, lean, Mr. Rook. The turkey pastrami's probably not turkey either."

Rook took his sandwich and soda back to the office. The elevators were running again, but there was a backlog and the lobby was jammed. He took a bite of the almost Jewish pickle.

"Smells good enough to eat," said the new tenant who looked like Cybill Shepherd.

"It's my cologne," he told her.

She winked and followed the next group on to the elevator.

The phone was ringing when Rook got up to his office. It was Everett Warden. "Don't come heavy," he said.

"Now, there's a term I haven't heard since *The Godfather*."

"Actually, *The Sopranos*, episode 4, I believe, Mr. Rook. Junior's talking to Tony over a plate of pasta."

"I think they call it 'macaroni,' Dick, and they're not such entertaining folks."

"You'll have to tell me about that sometime," said Warden. "In the meantime, please do leave your firearm at home. Insurance considerations, you understand."

"Sure I do. No problem."

Right, no problem carrying anything that shows. A problem is you need something it's somewheres else. The .38 snubby if the rented monkey suit doesn't hang right.

The phone rang again. It was Tom Bailey.

"How's it hanging, Rook?" he said.

"It's hanging. How's my favorite movie star?"

"Still driving. You know I got what they call a 'call back' but one of them casting people said I didn't look menacing enough. The other said I was too menacing. You know how that is."

"I guess I do," said Lucas. He took a bite of his sandwich.

"Anyways, you're interested, I got some work for you for a change. I get a call for my car service. Some 'honorary consul,' whatever that is, looking for somebody to babysit him while he's in town for this Pennsylvania Weekend circle jerk."

"Depends on the time, Tom. Friday and Saturday nights are no good."

"Sorry, Rook, then maybe next time. How about after the holidays, we grab a beer?"

"Sounds like a plan," said Lucas and he got back to his corned beef on rye.

He was sopping up the last of the brown mustard when he got another call, but it was domestic relations work which is always shit. You're working for the husband, he's paranoid you don't find anything and a basket case you do. You're working for the wife, she wants you to bang her. You're working for the lawyer, he tries to fuck you too.

Lucas was out on to Fifth Avenue when his cell phone rang. It was Warden again. "Bring your report to date on the Maguire case," he said.

"You want to meet a half hour earlier or whatever?" Rook asked.

"That won't be necessary," said Warden and he hung up.

Lucas went back up to the office and looked at what he had. The way he'd handled the trip to San Fran and the possible new beneficiary was decent, mentioning only that the other kid had died and leaving out the date of death. No way they're not going to throw a shit fit he spent their hard-earned chasing a lead that was old and cold. He also gave them a taste of the mafia-Westies stuff on Anthony D'Angelo as a distraction.

Rook headed over to see the Hell's Kitchen jerkwads to get

some more billing in case Dickie had pulling the case in mind. He took his big .45 and his back-up piece. You go back to see Reds Maguire and Eddie Kelly, you do go heavy.

19

Rook sat on the Bobbsey Twins' apartment building, waiting for Eddie Kelly to leave so that he could have a little chat with Reds. Clinton Community Gardens was a good place to wait, a clear view of the building and good neighbors walking their dogs and picking up shit in little plastic bags. A woman in her 30s came up. "Will you sign the petition?" she asked. She made a good screen while she was standing there.

"Abolish the draft, legalize pot? What?"

" 'Save our Gardens.' The developers are coming in without any notice or redress."

"Tell me more and I'll think about it, but first tell me your name?" Lucas said. "I don't do solidarity with strangers."

The woman took a step back. "If you're going to sign, you can call me Flower."

"Your name is really Flower?" Rook asked.

"We're all children of the earth. We're all God's flowers," she said.

Ed Kelly came out of the apartment house. He flicked his cigarette butt into the street and went up the block like he wasn't something you picked up on the bottom of your shoe. His right hand was in his jacket pocket, which was either because of the beating he took or because he was carrying iron.

Lucas signed Kelly's name to the petition and went across the street. The doors to the building and the apartment were wide open. Reds Maguire was washing the dishes. He had an apron on.

"How nice, Reds. How very nice," said Rook.

Maguire reached for the knife on the drainboard, then turned around. "Look what the cat dragged in."

Rook sat down at the kitchen table. "You look just swell in your outfit."

"You got that check for me or the papers to sign, otherwise beat it."

"Things are a little more complicated, Reds, but that could be a good thing for you. Real good."

"You're talking about 'complications,' you're running a game. Sounds like old times." He turned around with the knife still in his hands.

Rook put his hand on the butt of his .45. "We do this any way you want," he said. "First thing is, I can show it was a pure accident, she wasn't drunk or anything, we're talking they pay double. AD&D, they call it."

Maguire put the knife down and took an unfiltered Kool from his apron pocket.

"Okay, Mr. Maguire. Let's do it the slow way. Your sister Helen fell down the steps and died. She either slipped and fell or somebody pushed her. There was a blood smear on the wall. She had two kids."

"She had one." He fired up his smoke.

There was a noise in the hall. Lucas turned his chair to triangulate Reds and Ed Kelly if he came in. A woman and a kid went by.

"Wrong, one son died in Iraq. She had another baby with her boyfriend, Reds, you know that. She gave the kid up."

"No good wop greaser." Maguire dropped his cigarette into the dish water. "Helen told me the baby died. So where's my double bubble, or you trying to fuck me?"

"There's a 'Slayer's Exception,'" Lucas said. "Which I'm not saying applies here. That's they won't pay if the beneficiary killed her."

Reds started for the knife, then stopped. "Meaning you think I pushed my own sister down the steps."

"I'm not saying that and I'm not thinking that. Except maybe you're both drinking, she got a temper…"

"Fuck you," said Maguire.

"I'm asking you if you know anybody who'd push Helen down the steps. Somebody had it in for her. Jealousy, whatever. Maybe Anthony, the boyfriend, somebody else. We got somebody else, it's not you. No exception or whatever. You're home free and we're talking they're paying you two times the fifty."

Reds squinted through his exhale. "That greaser's gone. Otherwise, it's him."

"She seeing anybody else, drinking with anybody regular? Maybe the taproom she went to."

"My sister had a drink or two, but she drank at home. Said it wasn't right a lady went into the bar unescorted."

"How about Eddie? He ever take her?"

Heavy footsteps came down the hall and the big man came in.

"What the fuck?" Eddie said.

Rook shifted his position again so he was ready for both of them. "Speak of the devil," he said.

Kelly started over fast. Rook stayed in the chair, but spread his stance and produced the Glock.

Kelly stopped in his tracks.

"This would make a hole coming out the size of your head, Eddie. Now sit down and shut up or go back out and walk around the block while we finish up."

"Go on," said Reds. "I want to hear what this jerk-off has to say."

"I ain't going nowheres," said Kelly.

Rook took a twenty out of his shirt pocket with his left hand. "It's on me," he said. "Shot and a beer. A six pack."

"We're not done," said the big man. "And stick your money up your ass."

"Go on, Eddie. I got business here," said Maguire.

Lucas reholstered his weapon when Kelly left. "You were telling me about your sister."

"No I wasn't. You're sounding more like a cop, so I ain't telling you shit."

"That's up to you whether you're talking or not. I was just asking about your sister."

"You've been talkin' about my sister who's dead. Maybe we should talk about your brother's dead. See if you like me talking about that."

"Fine with me, Mister I-could-have-had-it-made. You got nothing for me. I got nothing for you."

Reds lit another menthol. "I can give you this. Then we're done. Her 'boyfriend' was half a fag, that wop no-good. Otherwise, he wouldn't run out on her. No way he does nothing. Only person I ever know Helen had a bad word with was another dago, as a matter of fact. Johnnie Falco, ran the beauty shop she used to work at, Johnnie, he throws a fit she leaves and takes her book of business for her to do hair in her basement so she's not on the welfare or starving to death."

Rook got up. "Appreciate it. You're telling what taproom Helen had a Cosmopolitan at once in a blue moon, I'm out of here."

"The joint got a ladies' entrance. Around the corner from Sacred Heart. Now that's all except Helen drank, but wasn't no drunk, so you owe me double which you shouldn't have been keeping from me." Maguire exhaled streams of smoke from his nostrils. "Other than that, you can scram."

"Have a nice day," said Lucas Rook. "Lovely place you got here."

Ray Tuzio, who was now living in a world of strangers, rice pudding and his own shit, had taught Rook how to conduct an interview and what it told you. So the picture of Reds and his kitchen knife said a lot more than the bullshit about the beauty shop, which is telling only that there's some more billing to back in.

Ray also told him you follow the honey trail, which means pussy or money, which is enough on this job to take a look at Johnnie Falco. Maybe you're stealing customers was enough to get Helen killed.

Rook did his preliminary run on Falco. The beauty shop guy had a sheet twice for pot, but further sleuthing confirmed that Mr. Falco sold out to a chain of beauty shops called "Stars" a year before Helen Maguire's death and died of equine encephalitis shortly thereafter.

20

The Waldorf was still the Waldorf even though there were no longer white gloved attendants running the elevators. Instead there were inattentive security guards talking on their cell phones. Rook walked around the building before going in, more from habit than anything else. A cabbie and the doorman were trying to settle a dispute between a tall, palsied man who looked like Bert, the kids' puppet character, and a chubby Jewish guy trying to look Hollywood.

The lobby was filled with couples checking in and posing. Pennsylvania: Philly and Pittsburgh with Alabama in between. For more than a hundred years, the powerful and the want-to-be's had been coming to New York City the second weekend of December to shop, drink and cut their deals.

There was an endless string of cocktail parties thrown by the big law firms, and the corporations which produced lots of business to go with the holiday cheer and the opportunity for the politicians to show they could fundraise their asses off and drink beer from a bottle. With gambling coming to the Keystone State there was likely to be more than the usual number of secret meetings held under the cover of Broadway shows and the naughty forays to

Canal Street for knock-off handbags.

Rook walked past the loud party in the first floor ballroom. Somebody running for something with somebody else's money. The theme was nautical, a genius's idea for some sure press coverage, "Squid Pro Quo."

Down the marble stairs was the Bull and Bear, mostly empty except for a few losers and two sets of tourists. A Scandinavian family was arguing about something and three Indian couples were well on their way to getting drunk. A woman in dark glasses and a cape walked through, muttering something about LA and her grandfather.

Lucas sat at the bar and had himself a bottled beer. He checked his watch. Everett Warden should be coming in any minute. Being the asshole he is about time, no way is he going to be late. Twenty minutes and another beer later, Rook's phone rang.

"I'm sorry to put you out," said Warden. "Home Office just left. Their end of the year audit went a little longer than we anticipated."

"We still in business?"

"Of course we are, Mr. Rook. The audit went quite well in fact, although I myself had some concern about your billing practices."

"I meant our meeting this evening."

The insurance man actually laughed, a pinched, nervous laugh, but a laugh nonetheless. "Of course you did, and so did I. Insurance humor, we call it. Actually, things turned out quite well, the meeting I had scheduled for tonight has been pushed back to tomorrow at two-thirty, so I won't be needing you tonight. I trust you can make it tomorrow, unless you have plans for a Broadway matinee."

"She lives on the East side, Mr. Warden, and her husband will be home."

Warden waited, trying to figure it out. Then he did. "Matinee is the key word. Romantic interlude in the middle of the day. Private investigator humor, I take it."

Lucas finished his beer. "Exactly."

"I'll meet you in the bar off the lobby at one-thirty to prepare."

Rook signaled the bartender for another. "And tonight?"

"Our agreed-upon rate or any hours you may legitimately be putting in on the Maguire assignment, which should be winding up. But not both."

"Of course not, Mr. Warden. I'd never think of it." Of course not. You're selling your time and you're lucky enough to have multiple assignments, you stack them up like planes at La Guardia. The secret is not to be stupid about it.

The bar was filling up. The men in new striped suits. The girls smart enough to appreciate the stratagem of the blowjob as corporate politics. The Scandinavian family had calmed themselves with chocolate desserts. The Indians were getting rowdy. "New Delhi in the house," yelled one. "Bombay represent," yelled another. Somewhere that non-violence guy in diapers was turning over in his grave.

Rook went outside. The line for cabs was long and treacherous. A college kid with one of those pedal rickshaws called out, but Lucas waved him away.

The couple of beers had done the bad leg some good, but 5th Avenue would be a mess with the holiday crowd. Rook walked east and got a taxi at Third Avenue.

"You want me to go up to Columbus Circle?" asked the cabby.

"No and it's not Avenue of the Americas either, pal."

"Right, right, you're from here. I could tell anyway."

"Sure you could, pal. And don't block the box or whatever, either."

Rosen's garage was closed, but there was a light on in the back. Lucas used his key. There was music, forties crooner stuff.

"It's just me, Sid. I'll take the Merc."

Rosen came out from the back. "You thought I was entertaining a lady with my Vaughn Monroe?"

"Could have been. Going out to see Tuze."

"Better I need to get my joint copped, I go get a little wishy-washy than bring them home. They stay more than twenty minutes, they think they're *mishbukah*."

"That means 'family' or 'bankrupt,' right, Sidney?"

"Right, Lucas boy. I'll ride out with you," said Rosen. "We can stop for some barbecue on the way back. I got this Towne Car to test drive."

The same sawed-off rent-a-cop was outside. "Visiting hours are over," he said. Then he recognized Rook. "Sure, sure," he added. "But could your friend move his vehicle in case we need to…"

" 'Vehicle,' you say. That's police talk, isn't it? Sure he will, but only if he needs to. I won't be long." Just long enough to see that Tuze was alright and remind them not to treat him like a dog. The only report he was going to make is putting hands on somebody if Ray Tuzio was tranqed out or whatever. Tuze wasn't, but he just as well might have been. He was sitting in a hard-backed chair, drooling into his shirt.

"You alright, partner?" Rook asked him.

Tuze didn't answer.

Lucas looked for his aviator glasses. They were in Ray's little bureau along with a cake of soap. So maybe these little visits were paying off.

The patient in the bed next to them sat up. "We're going, we're going," he said, then he went back to sleep.

A new pretend nurse came in. "There are no visiting hours now," she said.

"How's my uncle doing?"

"He's doing fine. You should be leaving."

Rook ignored her.

"I'll be back in ten minutes," she said.

Lucas helped Ray Tuzio to the bed and covered him up. "You need anything, Tuze," Lucas said, "I'll be here in a heartbeat."

"He alright?" Sid asked when Rook got back into the car.

"Fuck me," Lucas told him.

"You want to skip the barbecue?" Sid said. "I know a good saloon on the way back."

"Good idea," said Rook.

They stopped for a couple at a place called the Bywood Tavern. Good place. Nobody bothered nobody. Lucas drank until the alcohol caught up with his memories and then went back to his apartment.

His cell phone rang at one-thirty in the morning. It was Everett Warden and he sounded scared to death.

"I'm in trouble and you've got to get me out of it."

"What kind of trouble, Mr. Warden?"

"Talk to the detective, Mr. Rook. He wants to…"

Detective Nucifora took the phone. "Is that you?" he said. "I thought I was going to be talking to some high-priced lawyer."

"Nucie. What you got?"

The big detective waved Warden away. "Friend of yours, Lucas?"

"Not hardly, but I'm working for him."

"Mr. Warden here's frequenting the services of an underaged for illicit purposes. The pros, she's only fifteen."

"You working vice since how long?" Rook asked.

"Couple months. Good working with you on that funeral parlor job."

"Can you give my employer some rhythm here? He's such a nice boy."

"I'll take care of it, but let me scare the creep some more, he being the rude cocksucker he is and not even taking his socks off for the lady. Those fancy socks too, what do you call them?"

"Argyles, I think."

"Right, argyles. Here's Mr. Fancy Socks."

Everett Warden got on the phone.

"Am I going to be alright? I get arrested and I'm done. And you know I…"

"You keep talking, you're talking your way into something."

"Okay, okay."

"Alright, Mr. Warden. And what about tomorrow?" asked Rook.

"I'm getting out of here."

"And?"

"I'll pay you for the assignment."

"And?"

"You can take your time with the Helen Maguire case. Just don't make me look bad."

"You do that yourself, Mr. Warden. Now I'm going back to sleep. Without my fancy socks on."

21

The insurance company rings the dinner bell, you're stupid not to waddle up for another course, which meant a day plus or minus on the son who died in Iraq and some on the kid who died.

Lucas Rook was drinking coffee and surfing the net for billables on An Najaf, where Helen Maguire's kid got killed, when the phone rang. It was Wingy. "And how are you, my friendly friend?" asked Rosenzweig.

"I'm fine, my friendly friend. To what do I owe this fine call?"

"For a game of canasta and some Mexican. I miss your charming company."

Rook knew the drugman made a call, it wasn't for an evening of good fellowship.

"See you within the hour, Wingy." You get a call like that from somebody like Wingy Rosenzweig, you do him the solid and give him what you can.

Lucas Rook did a little more research before he left to see his drug-dealing friend. George W declared the end of major combat on May 1, 2003. Helen's kid gets turned into chili two years to the day, Happy Anniversary. He also found that Captain Arthur Blessing, whose interview Mr. Warden had made appropriate with his call for help at one AM, was still at Fort Hamilton, a trip he'd make after he took care of Wingy.

There was the usual security at Wingy Rosenzweig's front door and upstairs, but this time the barking dog was real. Wingy looked glad to see him, but the Rottweiler didn't appear to share the sentiment.

"Sit, Babe, sit."

The dog didn't. Wingy kicked him in the flank. Babe sat.

"Your dog doesn't seem to like me, Wingy. I would have hated to have shot him without first being properly introduced."

Wingy sent the dog to his crate.

"He's not anti-anything. He's just a dog that thinks he's a badass. That's why we get along."

The door buzzer rang. Rosenzweig went to the intercom.

"You can come up," he told the deliveryman. "Yeah, right, I got the dog put away."

Rook sat down. The place was the same except for the picture of Wingy and his wife that used to be there, looking happy as clams in their Hawaiian shirts, Mrs. R tan and fit, Wingy smiling like a jackass and waving to the camera with his flipper arm.

The drug dealer didn't miss a thing, including Rook's glance to where the photo used to be.

"Come on," he said. "I'll show you."

They went into the bedroom where Wingy kept a street-sweeper shotgun and his drug safe. There on the ceiling was a life-sized painting made from that photo.

"You're thinking I'm crazy having the picture of her and me like that. Only way I can sleep is looking at the wife."

The front door rang. The dog went nuts.

"Let me leave it," said the delivery boy. "You can give them your credit card."

"I'll do that. With the tip," said Rosenzweig.

The drug dealer served the food.

"You got something for me?" Rook asked.

"I do, Lucas, I do. The girl comes over to give me blowjobs has a son got himself jammed up."

He wrote down her phone number. "Her name is Sarah. Nice lady. Except for the fact that she's making her living swallowing jism."

Lucas read the number and handed back the piece of paper. "I'll see what I can do."

They both knew he would and that whatever trouble the kid had got himself in would be straightened out if it wasn't fucked-up bad.

"You can charge her," said Rosenzweig.

"Appreciate that," said Lucas. "I'll treat her right."

"I know you will," said Wingy. "I know that."

They finished eating and Rook headed out. He thought about stopping by the office, but called Captain Blessing from his cell.

A Latin girl answered the phone.

"Detective Lucas Rook for the captain."

"May I ask the purpose of your call?"

"Tell Art it's about our golf outing."

She put him through.

"Minority hiring?" Lucas asked.

"You have no idea," said the head of the Criminal Investigation Division. "What can I do you for?"

"I'm working on something. It won't take long."

"Today?" asked the captain. "I can hear you're moving."

"That would be good, Art."

"Two o'clock."

"Two o'clock," said Rook.

No cop wants to travel where he doesn't have control, like taking the R train and the B-8 bus. Lucas got his Merc from Sid's

garage and took the Verrazano Bridge to the FHP. Since he was on
the clock, the ride was not a pain in the ass even though there was a
back-up at the 92nd Street exit.

Security at Fort Hamilton, "The Army's Ambassador to New
York City," was only for show. The welcoming sign announced,
"The Fort's image is to transform Fort Hamilton into a state-of-
the-art support platform, responsive and relevant to the needs of
our stakeholders."

It was good to sit down with Art Blessing. The captain was the
real deal, combat Airborne, and then intelligence. He joined the
Criminal Investigation Command and worked his way up the ladder
from special agent to operations officer and was now running CID
out of Fort Hamilton. He was wearing an eye patch and chewing on
a plasic straw when Rook came in.

"Don't I cut a dashing figure," he said. "Sorry to hear about
your brother."

They shook hands and sat down.

"What's that old saying, Lucas? 'Retaliation is the best cure'?"

"How you doing, Captain?"

Blessing dropped the straw in the trash. "We're a tobacco-free
zone here. So I want to smoke a cigar, I got to go outside."

"I saw the Command's photos when I came," Lucas said.

The captain leaned forward. "Don't get me started, but that's
'Today's Army.' I'm sure it's gotten to NYPD."

"You bet, LEO 24/7, Arthur."

"LEO?"

"Law Enforcement by Oprah."

Captain Blessing adjusted his patch. "Meanwhile, this WMD
doesn't respond, I'm into civvies anyway. 'Wet Macular Degenera-
tion' it stands for, I know there's a joke somewhere. Meanwhile,
until I'm blind as a bat, the eyepatch is 'dashing,' I think they say."

"It was good working with you, Captain," said Lucas. "The
Latin Kings."

"Roger that. We got a hundred of those animals, including

King Tone."

"Antonio Fernandez, the 'Primero Corona,' the First Crown."

"And by animals, detective, I was referring to their gang chapters, the Tiger Tribe, Wolf Tribe, and so on."

"Of course you are, Captain."

"Of course, otherwise I'd be out of step with some new directive from my CO, 'Commanding Oprah,' I guess you'd say." He took a cigar from his desk. "What can I do for you, Rook?"

"I'm private now. Working for an insurance company on this assignment. Lady falls down the steps and becomes dead. Her son predeceased her." He looked in his narrow spiral notebook. "KIA, 1 May 05. His DD214 was in his mother's records. I'm looking for whatever else there is."

"I'm supposed to tell you make a request under the Freedom of Information and Privacy Act."

Lucas waited for him to go on.

"Remember that restaurant, detective?"

"La Hacienda?"

"No, the other one. Tomorrow 1700."

Rook left the base, glad he had driven. The storm was coming down hard and cold.

Captain Blessing stepped out and lit his cigar. He leaned against his building and sent smoke rings into the rain.

22

When Rook got back to his apartment at the St. Claire, there was a plastic bag hanging on his door. Two oranges and a banana. It's a phallic joke gift, it must be Grace Savoy. Lucas rang her bell.

"You looking for the Welcome Wagon lady?" she asked.

He handed her the bag of fruit. "You shouldn't open the door before you know who it is."

"My peephole doesn't work and neither do my peepers. And anyway, you forgot, I can hear a pigeon fart a mile away."

Grace went over to the abacus on the black and white kitchen table. "Did you figure it out, neighbor?" she said.

"What are we talking about, Gracey? The fruit salad hanging from my door?"

"Carmen Miranda wore those fruit hats. She died on stage of a heart attack." Grace started to cry. "She was only 46, a heart attack. Carmen was with Jimmy Durante when she died. Inka-dinka-doo."

She lit a cigarette and began sliding the beads on the abacus. "The average price of an apartment in New York is $1.5 million, which is a forty percent increase over October 2004. The price per square foot in Manhattan is $1200."

"So the douche bags who've been sneaking around the building are going to turn this condo," Rook said.

"You got it, neighbor. I met with the real estate agent who's going to be handling the pre-sale. Evelyn Graf. She seemed nice enough."

Grace went back to her abacus and made the beads fly across the wires. "This is from the numbers she gave. Figuring just under $1.2 million with a monthly maintenance, you put down twenty percent, the monthly is $3,716."

"Sure it is."

"Or another way to look at it is you have $900 common charges, monthly taxes around $500, it's going to run a little under $7000 per month with 10 percent down."

"Terrific, Gracey, that's just swell."

She snubbed out her menthol. "Of course, they're going to give some kind of deal for prior occupants."

"Of course they are. 'They,' whoever they are, going to pay my moving expenses out to Queens, which is where I'm going at those numbers?"

"You want to talk about this?" she asked him.

"What's to talk about at those numbers?"

"Okay, so you're a man of action, not a man of means. And I'm your blind, hot blonde girl next door who's got a knack for numbers and a pussy ring with cat's eyes on it."

"The image is too much for me to comprehend, Gracey."

"But not the numbers, dear." She clicked the abacus again. "I buy the joint, you pay the monthly maintenance, I finance the rest to you."

"That's good, Ms. Savoy. How about a term of about six hundred years?"

"We can work this out. You get some equity. Maybe you'll find a pot of gold or some treasure trove on one of your cases or you get a big reward for bringing a bad guy, like Osama."

"The numbers you're talking, I better bring him in handcuffed to Pontius Pilate."

Grace lit another cigarette. "Most of all, you don't have to move. I need you here, Lucas. I need you right next door." She stood up. "And right now I need you to take me about for a pork sandwich and a beer."

"Deal, Gracey. That I can do."

They walked the six blocks to "Prince of Pork" and ordered take-out, which they ate at the bolted-down pink picnic tables.

"I want to thank you about the Iris Society," Grace said. "Not getting my money, I do appreciate that, but more than that."

"I understand. Old friends can do bad things, Gracey."

She picked a piece of provolone. "And the good guys. The Montclair Council has been very supportive and the police don't think I'm batshit."

She took his hand, then kissed it. "And you're the best of all. You make me exquisitely happy."

"If you say so."

"Hugo did, Lucas Rook."

"Hugo who?"

"Victor Hugo said, 'To be blind and to be loved is indeed, upon this earth where nothing is complete, one of the most strangely exquisite forms of happiness.' And do you know what the other ones are, Lucas?"

He sopped his bread and took another drink of beer. "I'm sure you'll tell me."

"You riding me like a bucking bronco and telling me you've sent all the bad guys to hell where they belong."

"All of them is a lot, Gracey."

When they got back to the St. Claire, Grace Savoy invited him in, but Rook told her he had work to do. He did Internet research on a seven-year-old who had died away from home, while Grace smoked a joint and masturbated herself to sleep.

Lucas had his notes from his interview with Anthony D'Angelo and worked the follow-up. Helen Maguire had her baby and gave it to Catholic services, who placed him for adoption. Years later, that prince of a man, John Gotti, used his Mafioso skills to find the kid, a huge deal at that time, and then the boy dies.

Rook got all he needed with the computer and the phone. Young Anthony was buried in the Sacred Hearts of Jesus and Mary cemetery. His parents were Michael and Nancy Luongo of Yaphank, Suffolk County. The father worked at Long Island Copy Service. The mother at the C.E. Walters School. The kid died at Long Island Jewish Medical Center of acute myelogenous leukemia, AML. WebMD said that was the second most common pediatric leukemia. The Irish mother's kid gets raised by Italians and dies in a Jewish hospital. God bless America.

It was just after midnight, but who could sleep with all that joy in his head. A night like this, when you're working a dead kid after your blind neighbor tells you you don't have a pot to piss in, is going to make you feel like punching somebody's lights out. Another option is a blowjob from Valerie Moon or a long walk with Catherine. Neither was going to be thrilled to get a midnight call from somebody who wasn't the best at keeping his feelings from coming through. In the good old days, you rolled by maybe one of the clean houses on the Upper East Side and got a good fuck without your dick falling off afterward. But that was when loyalty meant something and it didn't cost you a thousand bucks.

Rook did some push-ups and had a beer. He wrote up his report on Helen's kid. Then he had another beer and went back onto the Web and accessed the Municipal Credit Union to maybe do a mortgage application. The site said that you could call for an application or go over to the Lafayette Street office.

Lucas looked at the monthly rate and payment calculator they had on the web site. Thirty years you're paying $6.16 per thousand dollars borrowed. You pay two points it goes down to $5.84 per thousand. Cashing in what savings he had wouldn't be enough to cover the down payment and would leave him hanging over the edge. There was always Kirk's Avanti, which could bring him somewhere in the 20's. So maybe Grace fronts him the down money and he gets the mortgage.

The credit union opened at eight, but that wasn't going to happen, and the Westsider trying to cash in on his sister lying at the bottom of the stairs was coming in at eleven. At least for Reds Maguire you didn't have to spit and polish the office.

Right now his cholesterol could go fuck itself. He made himself some salami and eggs. Lucas poured himself the almost last beer of the day and turned on the boob tube. *Cinderella Man*. Great flick that didn't get a sniff at the box office. They should've had it he dressed like Cinderella when he got home, that would have won an Oscar.

Rook fell asleep on the sofa, which is what God invented them for, and got through without having to get up to take a piss. There was a dream, there always was, but this time they were both eleven years old and driving their father's big DeSoto, only in the dream it was the Avanti also somehow. Then they somehow got separated and he was looking for the car and Kirk, but he couldn't find them no matter what he did and then it started to rain but it wasn't raining rain, it was raining round, white stones which hurt like hell and made a thunderous noise.

The sound was someone knocking on the door. "It's building management, Mr. Rook. I tried the phone, but no one answered."

"I must have unplugged it, telemarketers."

"It's Evelyn Graf too, from the realtor, Mr. Rook. I spoke to your neighbor, Ms. Savoy."

"Give me a half-hour, forty-five minutes."

"I have a busy schedule," said Ms. Graf.

"I've got two bad guys cuffed to the radiator, people."

"He's a detective," the manager said.

"Give me twenty minutes and I'll have these two desperados out of here," Lucas told them.

The realtor slipped her card under the door. Glasses, a nice smile. Rook cleaned a piece of salami from between his teeth and put the card on the counter. Then he showered and went out to do a bunch of things that were a pain in the ass.

The credit union was jammed. Staples didn't carry the toner that he needed for his printer.

Rook went up to the office and read the *Post* and the *Daily News*, then he moved some papers around and called the credit union to mail a mortgage app. Then he called Rosen too just to see what he could get for the Avanti. Sid's answering machine was on. "Your vehicle will be ready when I said it was. I do not accept personal checks."

23

Reds Maguire didn't show for his eleven o'clock, which meant not only the billing was gone, but he had cleaned up the pizza boxes for nothing. The phone rang.

There's good news over the phone, it's more than likely a wrong number. So it was like pigs could fly when Hugh Sirlin's secretary called. "Mr. Sirlin asked me to relay that it is in regard to a new matter."

Rook had done the "hearse ghoul" job for the big funeral corporation on East 42nd, and he had obviously done it right enough that maybe SDA wanted another "seamless transition." Lucas changed into the pants from his black suit and put on an almost matching turtleneck to give that *Spenser for Hire* look and coordinate with that black wall behind his fancy desk that Sirlin should get smacked for.

If it wasn't for the promise of green coming with it, the décor of SDA would be too much. The black front of the building, Ms. Marble's phony black glasses, the black wall behind Hugh Sirlin's black desk. Except Ms. Marble and her Canadian accent weren't there. A blonde, Eastern European, with high cheekbones and strong hands. Her compassionate affect was no doubt as practiced as her English.

"You must be Mr. Rook," she said. "Mr. Sirlin's expecting you." She looked at her computer screen. "He will be with you shortly."

"And your name is?" Lucas asked her.

"I am Mr. Sirlin's secretary," she told him.

"Certainly you are, dear. I'll be happy to entertain myself with your thoughtful brochures."

Sirlin kept him waiting forty-five minutes, which only works for doctors or jitbags who are going to write you big checks.

"Sorry, Mr. Rook. It's one of those days," said the fit-looking man in the somber, but elegant clothes.

The mystery lady led them to a small conference room to the right.

"I thought you'd find this more comfortable, Mr. Rook," Hugh said.

So Sirlin had noticed that he didn't like it that the wall in his office hinted at the Vietnam Memorial. Maybe after the meeting he'd give out a lollipop or whatever.

"I'm glad you could make time for me on such short notice, Mr. Rook. But I should not be surprised." He looked at the file waiting for him. "Professional and accommodating."

"I do what I can, Hugh."

Sirlin smiled at Rook's reference to the last job, in which SDA did the hard work in-house and Rook just made it kosher.

The secretary came back in with a tray of water.

"Thank you, Marlena," said Sirlin.

"Thank you, Marlena," said Rook.

The SDA executive poured himself a Pellegrino. "Another unseemly circumstance," he said.

"Not another one of your people depositing himself on the dearly departed."

"No, no, but just as distasteful, I'm afraid." He took a tasteful sip of the bubble water. "What did you call that last situation, 'the hearse ghoul'? Well, I'm afraid that 'ghoul' is not so hyperbolic this time. As I'm sure you've read or heard, there are serious allegations against funeral homes and tissue procurement services as to illegally harvesting body parts and selling them to health providers for implant procedures."

"Like that television host."

"That's the allegation," said Sirlin, "that Alistair Cooke had his bones and tissue sold to a tissue bank. The man was 95, for heaven's sake, which is ten years older than the limit for donations. Not to mention that he died of lung cancer which had metastasized to his bones. A woman in New Jersey is alleging she contracted syphilis from another graft. There's other such concerns in Pennsylvania, Florida and Texas."

"Brooklyn DA's looking at this Mastromarino character for organlegging, which is what us cops call stealing body parts."

"You know the case?" asked Sirlin.

"Just a little chit-chat and what I read about in the papers. I hear they exhumed some bodies and out in Queens somebody had replaced this eighty-year-old lady's legs with plastic plumbing pipe. It's going to be a field day for the PI lawyers at the least."

Sirlin sipped his water. "The worst kind of grave robbers. We can deal with them."

"SDA has what, three thousand locations?"

"I'm flattered you remembered," said Sirlin. "Actually, the numbers fluctuate."

The executive slid his chair back from the table. "We're clean as a whistle. You're familiar with our security program. What I am interested in is a liaison with the authorities. There's the Brooklyn, Manhattan DA's, the police department and so on."

Lucas took a drink of the Pellegrino. "Not if I'm just for show, Mr. Sirlin. I'm happy to help you coordinate things and I'm probably going to know a good number of whoever's working the case, but last time I was here was as far as I go. Obstructing is not my cup of tea."

Hugh Sirlin smoothed his black silk tie. "Of course not. What

I, Corporate, is thinking about is a retainer of fifteen hundred dollars a month. An hourly rate of $110. You'll be working with Ms. O'Reilly, you remember her. Anything delicate, you'll report directly to me. If I am not here, she will know where to find me."

"You're talking the possibility of anything 'delicate,' we're talking an additional five hundred per week, plus reasonable expenses. Anything over a hundred, I get prior approval."

"We have your W-9. As you will be going on retainer, we have different procedures. I'll see that you have our standard agreement and an initial check within twenty-four hours." Hugh Sirlin stood up and offered another one of his understanding handshakes. "It will be nice to be working with you again."

Marlena came in to usher Lucas out and pretended she was not an annoying twat.

A good phone call and a good meeting. The coinage could be serious, which couldn't come at a better time.

On the cab back downtown, Lucas played with the numbers again of what it would take to get his apartment. If he could turn this thing with SDA into something long-term, maybe the credit union could do something for him so he could do the deal without Gracey. If he needed it, maybe Rosenzweig would give a hand, although with Wingy that wasn't so easy to do.

Lucas stopped at the office to start his new file and get some billing in with computer research, which would appear on the invoice as "field work." Mastromarino used to be a dentist. There was Joseph Nicelli, an embalmer. There was a thing in Philly.

Found a couple of movies about organlegging, *Freejack* and *Seconds*. Also that human spines brought five grand on the black market.

The phone rang. It was Wingy Rosenzweig. "Never mind on that thing, Lucas."

"You sure?" Rook said. "I got a call in."

"Sure, I'm sure. Sure as my drippy dick. Her bastard kid can die. I'm taking ofloaxin, she's taking a walk. Appreciate it anyway."

"Sure, Wingy. No problem. I might be down your way anyhow."

"Bring some hot pastrami, Lucas. It cures everything."

"Done deal," said Rook.

"Done deal," said Rosenzweig.

Rook stopped by the shoeshine stand, but his browns were not back yet from the shoe repair.

"They have no respect for shoes," said Jimbo. "You got to respect what you do."

"I'll be by tomorrow, Jimbo. No sweat."

"With them tomatoes?"

"I'll see what I can do," Rook told him.

What he could do was run the iron over the gray pants for his next meeting. He was no clothes horse, but you don't have to be in *GQ* or whatever to know you don't wear suit pants too much that they're not matching the jacket anymore.

Lucas showered, changed and headed over to the Village to meet Captain Blessing. When he got to the restaurant, the place was closed, the captain was in civvies and half lit.

"Shut for renovations," he said. "And me, I'm wearing my fancy eye patch."

"I got just the place, Cap," Rook said. Get Art Blessing over to Hell's Kitchen and do some double-billing. He hailed them a cab. The taxi driver was some kind of Middle Eastern.

The captain waved him away. It took them two more taxis, but Blessing did allow a Sikh, "because they hate the towelhead camel fuckers almost as much as I do."

They got out at 52nd and 9th, where Rook had Coppersmith's in mind. Pictures of the New York skyline mounted on brick walls, lots of TV's, and the women and the bathrooms didn't make you want to puke. Captain Blessing steered them into El Azteca.

"Serving the Food of the Gods to the Children of the Gods."

"Good place for me to hide I like pretty colored drinks," the captain said. "Besides, anybody that tore little virgins' hearts out is my kind of place."

"I hear you," said Rook.

He heard a lot of other stuff too, but not about Helen Maguire's kid. The captain was pounding down Cosmopolitans and smoking cigars and laughing so loud about chicken fingers and something to do with getting the bad guys to talk, that the bouncer came over. A big, ugly-looking black guy who went half a fag when Blessing pulled up his shirt to show a wound that looked like Dr. Frankenstein did the surgery. "You want one?" Blessing said over and over so that Lucas had to find them a different watering hole.

The captain was still at it by the time they were in the back room at McCoy's where nobody seemed to give a shit. "On S and D forever," Blessing said. "Search and Destroy from here to the end of time and back again."

When he got even too loud for McCoy's, the barkeep had to tell him to tone it down. Blessing gave him a look he didn't want to see, not to mention flashing his survival knife. Rook took him out of the place.

"Sorry, detective," the captain said. "Got a case of the incomin'-outgoin'-shitkickin'-heartbreakin'-mama cryin'-choir singin'-puckered asshole-help me sweet Jesus-nobody's home blues. It happens from time to time when I've had too much alcohol. Your kid, the Maguire kid, KIA by the Al-Sadr militia, small arms fire at a food storage site. I looked at everything, AR casualty report, medical records. Some background too, although it had nothing much to do with him. Good kid, nothing much to mention, except he liked to gamble, dice, Internet poker. We looked at the gambling, anything like that it could cause a problem, especially when it was around supplies. He was a good kid. Is a dead kid." Blessing reached for a cigar, but he was out. "Truth and death, or maybe the other way around."

Lucas Rook put him in a cab back to Fort Hamilton and then went back into McCoy's to take a piss. Then he sat at the bar and had another draft.

As he was leaving, Reds Maguire came in. He was staggering drunk.

"I was just leaving," Lucas said. "You're only twelve hours late and you got the wrong place."

"I lost my appointment book, Rook, and no way was I doing anything but getting some beers, since all you do is blow smoke."

"Let's get our business settled so I don't have to see you anymore, Reds."

"It's my money," said Maguire.

"Sure it is. And right now I'm waiting on you."

Maguire put the six-pack under his arm. "Tomorrow afternoon," he said.

"One o'clock," said Rook. "And if your roomie's outside tell him he even looks in my direction, I'll break his other arm. It's been a long night and I'm not my charming, happy-go-lucky self."

24

Reds Maguire started the next morning like he did all the others, by lighting his first cigarette while he was still in bed. Eddie Kelly was gone to the world, sleeping on the pull-out and snoring like a subway. Reds went in to put a pan of water on to make a cup of coffee. He lit another smoke off the range and went to take a piss. He'd see Rook today, but you come running every time he calls, you look like a punk.

The two half-breed kids came running down the hall making a shitload of noise. Maybe he should go out without his teeth in and scare the Holy Christ out of them.

He combed his hair with a couple of drops of Wildroot which you could hardly get anymore. *"It's Wildroot cream oil, Charlie"* they would sing on the radio.

Eddie came into the bathroom. "I ain't going to crap," he said.

"When you do, open up the window," Maguire told him. "You're burning the paint off the walls."

It used to be he had a couple of runs to make. In the good old days Reds Maguire was collecting numbers or standing in to do some collecting if somebody was jammed up, taking a pinch, or sick or something. A couple of times he got to drive for one of the crew who was higher up. And he had done that one job, putting one behind the fat fuck's ear. But that was before Rudy Giuliani, that wop motherfucker, and the Feds mostly busted up most of the Westside mob.

Pocket full of smokes, .22 in his pocket. Ready for the world. Reds went over to the post office to check his box. The SSI check was late again, and the rent bill, which included heat, was there. They knew not to slip it under the door no more or to try and find some excuse to use the pass key and come snooping around.

Over at Reds' foot doctor, they didn't keep him waiting because they knew better, and Doc Braslow, the son, not the father, checked him that the sore near his ankle was doing good, which it was. The nurse had him soak his feet in a whirlpool which they were supposed to do first and then Doc Braslow, the kid, came in and trimmed his toenails which they probably charged as a surgery.

"You're doing fine, Mr. Maguire. Although I'd prefer you'd wear the shoes I prescribed."

"I got them, Doc. I just ain't going to wear them."

"It would likely decrease the incidence of those wounds."

"Ain't got no wounds on my feet," said Reds. "Just wearing on my ankle. So thank you very much if I don't wear no retard shoes."

"As you wish, Mr. Maguire. See the girl on the way out to schedule your follow up."

"Sure," said Reds, which he did not do since she was on the phone talking to her girlfriend, a fat Jew bitch anyway.

He had two stops before going to see Rook. One was at Mary's, where you could get a decent coffee and a roll on the house since they were making their money pouring shots, which he had two of. The other was to try and return the orthopedic shoes.

Manny's kid was running the building at 166 Fifth Avenue while his father was away.

"Pop said I had any questions, maybe you could help instead

of me asking that no good leech that sucked thirty grand from us for doing nothing."

"Lawyer takes your money and gets you a deal you could've gotten yourself's no surprise," Lucas told him.

"Right, what do you expect?" He adjusted his clip-on tie. "Pop gets eighteen months, he's going to do how many?"

"Federal time's pretty much straight time, so your dad does 15-16 months. Comes home looking better than when he left, fresh air, the treadmill, whatever."

Manny's kid just stood there. Lucas went into his office. Then the kid knocked and came in. "Thanks," he said. "I mean, I'll be working on your floor if you need anything, changing the locks on the restrooms. Got to make sure nobody sneaks in to take a shit that doesn't belong here."

Rook did some more housekeeping, which meant culling some of the newspapers from his office and chucking them into the incinerator room. On the way back, he saw somebody come out of the firestairs. Not Reds Maguire, but a black guy. Bad coming off of him and looking a lot like that Tyree Rollins years ago, who killed his girlfriend's child by holding the three-year-old's face into a birthday cake.

"Got the wrong place, my bad."

"Wrong place, wrong building, wrong city," Rook told him.

"You getting up in my grille?"

"Wolf somebody that gives us shit unless you want to go back inside."

The man turned to leave.

"Now wait a minute, homeboy. I'm going to ride down with you. Make sure you don't get lost," Rook said.

"I don't need…"

"Yes you do, my proud African friend. Unless you need to take a beating."

Rook rode him down on the service elevator. Manny's kid started in on the third floor, but Lucas waved him away and then pressed the emergency stop. He took out his big .45 and pointed at the black man's crotch. "We understand each other, nod your head." The man did. Lucas started the elevator up again. When they got to the ground floor, he walked him to the street. "Now have a nice day," he said.

The phone was ringing and the answering machine blinking when Lucas got back upstairs. Maybe the World calling to say thank you for streeting the shitbird from the building. The call was automated from his dentist's office, two reasons to hang up. The message was from Shirl Frelang to say thank you, which means that Warren G. Phelps, Esquire, had worked his magic once more, which was not to say that she didn't get banged on her bill.

The phone rang again. It was Valerie Moon, speaking of banging. "I'll be in the City this afternoon, handsome," she said.

"Lucky us," he told her.

"I thought maybe you can buy me a cocktail and give me some of the good stuff."

"Before or after?"

"Both, I hope. I can come by your office or you can meet me. I've got a gift certificate from Best of Scotland. I can put the sweater on and you can take it off."

"Sounds like a plan."

"Cashmere and my great cans. Life is beautiful. See you about four," Valerie said and she hung up.

A philosopher who'll suck her own nipples while you fuck her. What more could a man ask for? Ten of one. Time to get ready for that old Westsider. No such thing as a reformed shitbag. They get old, maybe they move a little slower and take more or less chances, depending. With Reds Maguire it meant he's trying to look like he wouldn't stab you in the back, but no way could you give him the chance.

Another phone call. Maybe that one line in the phone book between all those gigantic ads was really paying off. It was Catherine Wren.

"How are you?" she asked.

"I'm good, Cat."

"I miss you," she said.

"That's good."

"I'll be in the City. Father is taking me to the opera. I know how much you like that."

Somebody was at the door.

"Just a second," he told her. Rook opened his desk drawer so he could reach his Glock.

It was Manny's kid. "Thanks," he said. "For the advice and for throwing that piece of crap on the sidewalk. He came back in talking about suing and all, but I took Pop's pipe to him."

"Manny would be proud. I got a call, kid. Take it easy."

Lucas could hear Catherine smoking when he got back on to the phone, but let it pass. She runs, she watches her diet, she smokes. On the other hand, he loves her and is going to fuck Valerie Moon.

"I thought you could join us for a later dinner. I don't have any classes tomorrow. Then Daddy's car can take me back."

"Right," Lucas said. "Daddy's car."

Reds Maguire knocking on the door.

"I got to go, Cat. Daddy's car is fine."

"You sure?"

"I'm sure. And maybe he'll let me drive it someday. Wear a little cap."

"You'd look cute, Lucas."

"Never that, Catherine. I'll call you."

Reds had a cardboard box in his right hand when he came in. He put it down to serve the coffee.

"I got a bagel too," he said. "Which you're welcome to, me not being able to eat anything like that until I get my money to fix my teeth."

"Let's get to it," Rook said.

"I figure you had any other questions so you can finalize the paperwork, I'm here like you said."

Rook took half the bagel. "Right, Reds. I appreciate that."

Maguire reached for his smokes, but Lucas pointed to the sign on his desk. "No Smoking. It reminds me how much I miss it."

"Sure, sure. Only thing I got to say is that my sister had a very tough life. Tragic, you could say."

"Her death wasn't so easy either."

Reds drank some of his coffee. "Sure, sure. A tough life and death."

Lucas ate some of the bagel.

"So when are we talking about my insurance money, I mean?"

"Depends, Reds."

"Depends on shit. You know I didn't kill my sister. Nobody else did neither. That fall did, which means they owe me double."

"The insurance company hired me to do some work, Reds. I did it. They do all the rest."

Maguire started to stand up, then stopped. "I ain't giving you lip or nothin', I just want what's mine."

Rook pushed his chair back. "What's yours is yours, Reds, but the money doesn't come from me."

"You're fucking with me, right, holding up my money because of what you think I am and who you are, I mean who you was."

Lucas wiped his hands. "Let's try this again, Reds. I'm an investigator. I'm not an insurance company or a bank. I don't write checks and I don't hold them up. Other than that, I don't know what you're talking about."

This time Reds Maguire stood up. "This is chickenshit. I'm supposed to kiss your ass. I ain't got no beef with you, but I ain't no fag. You're sitting on my fifty grand, hundred grand and you're fucking with me because you used to be a cop. Well, I know cops. I knew your brother and other guys you know. Maybe better than you think I do."

Rook walked over slow. "I think we won't be seeing each other again, Reds. It won't be a good thing for you."

"I don't get my money, Rook, you'll be seeing me. And you

won't be sneaking me like you did Eddie. I'm better than that."

"Not good enough, Reds. Not nearly good enough. And you better pray you don't find that out. You better pray real hard."

25

Valerie Moon came by the office and stayed longer than usual because the real estate lady wanted to see Rook's apartment again. Let her deal with his boxers and towels on the floor while he had the pleasure of watching Valerie stand on his desk.

"Cashmere and my great cans like I told you, Lucas."

"You told me right."

"And my panties?" She unhooked her skirt. "Oops. I must have forgotten them."

"Come off of there before you fall," he told her.

Valerie Moon touched herself. "Why don't you take a seat at your desk and make sure I do."

There was a knock at the door.

"Go away," Rook told them. "I'm cleaning my gun."

"Mailman."

Rook went to answer the door and she got off the desk and folded her sweater neatly. He came back with two magazines and some circulars. "Dot head wanted me to sign for a letter that was supposed to go to the next floor. If I get the same friggin' mailman two days in a row it's a lot."

"Now where were we, Mr. Rook?" asked Valerie Moon. "I believe we were going to clean your gun."

When they were done, Rook walked to the bathroom in the hall and checked the place out before Valerie went in. He waited outside.

A fat lady came out of the office next door.

"Is everything alright?" she asked. "I heard noises."

"It is," said Lucas. "Dolly Parton's in there to powder her nose."

"Oh my," she said as Valerie came out. "Dolly Parton's in there powdering her nose."

"Is that a fact?" said Valerie. "I guess she must be sitting down to do the job."

They walked up Fifth Avenue. "I feel frisky, Lucas," said Valerie.

"Meaning what?"

"I feel frisky, Lucas, means I'm going to go up to Nine West and try on a hundred pair of boots."

"A hundred?"

"Or maybe fifty to go with my new cashmere."

Rook took her back down the block to the store at 10th Street. The manager was a striking redhead almost six feet tall. "I'll take this handsome couple," she told the salesgirl.

"Well, how can I help you two?"

"My niece here would like to try on fifty pair of boots, Tiffany, and I'd like to buy her thirty or so."

"Thirty is it? Well, we have a remarkable promotion going on. You don't buy one and you get one free. I'll be right back."

"Your niece, Lucas. I like that. It's so naughty."

The manager came back with a stack of boxes and presented them one by one.

"They're all perfect, how did you know?" said Valerie.

"That's what I do, dear," Tiffany said. "I think they're all lovely on you, but the first two are more perfect than perfect."

"You're absolutely right," said Valerie Moon. "Lucas?"

"Absolutely."

"Then absolutely it is," said the manager. "I'll have them bagged."

Rook reached for his wallet, but Tiffany shook her head.

"Well, that was something, Lucas," Valerie said when they got back onto the street.

"Nice girl, Tiffany. I helped him out once. Now let's get these boots their first shine by an expert."

"Only if I can model for you after lunch?"

"But of course, Valerie. Uncle Lucas would like that just fine."

They went to drop the boots off at Jimbo Turner's. The stand was covered with red paint, which the shineman was cleaning off with the turpentine he used for wiping down his shoes. He turned around when Rook came up.

"Now who could do this to a diabetic old white shineman?" he asked.

"You have any ideas, Jimbo?" Lucas asked.

"Maybe some vandals or some fools. I got this. Turp doesn't get it, the stand needs painting anyway. Hop on up. The lady can have my folding chair here."

"Got two pair to leave, Jimbo. I'll pick them up with my browns. The lady and I are going to lunch. I'll make a call over to the precinct and have the sector car keep an eye out."

The shineman nodded.

"And I'll see if the restaurant has the makings of a decent tomato sandwich, Jimbo," Lucas said.

"That was awful," Valerie Moon said as they walked away. "Who could do such a thing?"

He thought about Maguire at lunch, the jitbag leaving a calling card or whatever. Maybe it was paranoia or his basic distrust of everybody that breathed, but good cops don't believe in coincidence. And the red paint said "Reds Maguire" enough to let the mean out. That meant no encore with Valerie Moon and that he'd be paying the Hell's Kitchen piece of shit a visit he wouldn't forget.

Rook went back to his office alone and then went down to the basement to hit the heavy bag. Manny's son was in there banging away. Lucas slid in and held it for him, not saying a word except when the kid was done, that work gloves probably weren't the way to go. The kid was crying, and went upstairs.

Lucas made the 110-pound bag jump, working the body and the head, the head and the body. The more he hit it, the angrier he got. Reds Maguire, the fuckface Eddie Kelly, the prick insurance man, the wise-ass spade detective, Dwight Graves, who had jerked him around and busted his balls when Sid Rosen got beat, the real estate pricks making him move. And like always, the fucks who shot his brother dead.

So he was still angry at who killed his twin brother. Cholly the shrink would have fun with that. But Etillio and his gang wouldn't. They were all dead.

Lucas went back to his apartment and washed up. He did some work on the bone case. Get some billing in on that, move the numbers around on the apartment financing, have a couple of drinks so that when he went to dinner with Catherine Wren she wouldn't see the crazy man who was going to pay Reds Maguire a visit.

He had half-worked a blackmail body parts case when he was on the job. Working it with Hy Gromek before Hy got partnered up with that Cosby-looking, pompous black asshole Graves, whose only good thing was that Kirk had nothing bad to say about him when they worked together at the 7th precinct.

Hy and him had worked this African parking lot attendant named Duma who sold one of his kidneys so he would have enough money to bring his wife and daughter over. Probably so they could sell their parts to bring somebody else over and so on. Turns out the owner of the parking lots had something to do with it. Now Hy Gromek was dead. Too bad. He was a good cop and a good guy.

Rook turned on his computer. The term "organlegging" was apparently started by some science fiction writer named Niven, although there was nothing made up about stealing bones or body parts. There was a bigger demand because technology and demand meant bigger profit. This meant the Italian and the Russian mobs were in it for sure.

Within an hour, Lucas had a decent amount of spadework. He could take a look at Life Cell, which was described as legit, and Bio Medical Tissue Service that the news reports said wasn't. There also was Regeneration Services and the American Association of Tissue Banks, "providing a safe, adequate and affordable supply of tissues and cells." Lucas spent an hour reading up on those two, which yielded good billing and no indication of anything that had the stink on it.

To get the real skinny on what was going on, he called over to the Brooklyn DA. Finklestein was running out the door to do a preliminary hearing, but said they could meet "for a couple of belts" and told him that Luhtala was no longer investigating any-thing, having run off to Tibet with a performance artist, whatever that was, from the East Village.

Rook banded together his new stack of index cards and started on the projected budget for the job, not only for the client, but to help him with the credit union and then the real estate lady who had been stepping over his dirty towels and socks.

He had a beer and then took another shot at finishing the Ma-guire paperwork, but it just didn't go. Half because he needed the case to keep running and half because he was going to pay that visit, tuning the shanty-Irish, Westsider, washed-up, wannabe's ass up.

Lucas went back to his apartment building. The real estate lady was talking to the twins, who certainly had the coinage to buy their place, but she stopped for a moment to wave. "Looking forward," she said. Right, looking forward to what. She wouldn't be "looking forward" to talking to him at all if she knew better.

A shower and a beer later, he was alright and made his choice between *God's Grace*, which Rosen was busting his balls about re-turning, or *Hostage*. Sorry, Bernard Malamud, Bruce Willis just kicked your ass. But what can you say about the man who spoke those immortal words which still belonged on the dollar bill, "Cowboy the fuck up."

In the good old days you could get a bunch of posies and drink some fresh- squeezed orange juice at the stand on Greenwich Avenue as the unjustly convicted she-devils of New York threw toilet paper messages and hand signals from the Women's House of Detention. Now all of the Joan of Arc's were somewhere else and you're buying flowers and fresh-squeezed, you had to use your credit card. Thanks to the education he received from working that flower job for Gracey, Lucas was able to get a good deal on a bunch of irises. While maybe the colors didn't exactly go together, which the salesgirl told him, the names made up for it, "Golden Panther" and "Voodoo Magic."

Rook took his brother's Avanti out to keep it running and get a better idea of whether he could get rid of Kirk's car if he had to.

Catherine had the table set when he got there. "The flowers are beautiful," she said.

"Bearded and Aril," Lucas answered, but he wasn't sure that was right.

"I have wine in the fridge, but a man that brings a lady such beautiful and exotic irises deserves a cold beer."

He sat on the sofa. "And?"

"And, we'll see," she said from the kitchen. Rook called in to her that wine would be good.

The dinner was nice if you had just eaten or had your stomach stapled. Bib lettuce with pears and almonds, Cornish hen. She poured Lucas another glass of wine. "Sauvignon Blanc from Chile. Their wines are very healthy because of their level of flavanol, an antioxidant."

"It reminds me of the wine we had on the Square in Philly."

"You mean at that Italian restaurant, Lucas. The last time we didn't get much of a chance…"

He picked up his glass and put it back down. "Right, right. I forgot I pissed you off."

"For getting into a brawl," she said.

He sipped the wine. "I was the only one brawling."

"That's true."

"One of them had a knife, Catherine. They were predators hunting folks who looked weak."

"And instead they found somebody who saw red." Catherine got up. "Let me clear. I have coffee and dessert."

"Smart lady," Rook said as she left. Saw red. That's what I do. Sometimes it's right and sometimes it isn't. The red paint on Jimbo Turner's stand was most likely vandalism shit and not a calling card from the jitbag Maguire. The washed-up Westsider needed a beating, but on general principles. The beating he was going to get went on the shelf where there was plenty of inventory, and always room for one more.

Catherine Wren came out of the kitchen with meringue tarts and coffee that smelled like vanilla.

26

Grace Savoy called, begging, which was not the first time. Begging him to fuck her, begging him not to fuck her. Begging him to listen to some crazy story, like how her Uncle Bert was killed by lightning. Begging for him to come over and just sit with her, which he had done more than once, or like the time the red bird flew in off the patio and she killed it by accident and he had to describe it and give it a proper burial.

Probably a half dozen times he went over there across the low wall between their places or she came over, or they sat outside in the night. But never did he take her seeing-eye dog out to take a crap. There were the guys downstairs for that who did it for a fiver and maybe a peek at her tits.

Now since Gracey might be helping him with a swing loan or whatever, he did what she asked him to do. Lucas took the animal out. It even shit like it was working. "See, I'm taking a dump. I learned how to do it at Guidedog University."

One of the Department of Sanitation's finest hurried by as poochie was completing his performance. He had the look of I won't tell if you won't, going to or coming from something he wasn't supposed to.

"I saw that," said Rook's neighbor who had the big peanut on her cheek and always smelled like she had been drinking. "I'm going to report both of you. You for not curbing that dog and the sanitation worker who should have…"

"Sure you are," Rook told her. "You want me to wait while you pick up the evidence?"

"You could at least…"

Lucas offered her the leash. The dog didn't like it. "You want to take this too? I got to go help Manny, Manny's kid, unload the wine bottles from the incinerator room, on what floor is it, five?"

Grace was on her phone when he got upstairs.

"I don't think you understand. Or maybe you don't want to. Perhaps you'll be receiving a copy of my complaint to the Office on Human Rights Pat, Patricia Gatling herself helped me fill out. I'm blind, remember?"

She hung up and lit a cigarette. "How was that, neighbor?" she said.

"As impressive as Rin-tin-tin here taking a dump on the sidewalk."

"I appreciate that. I really do. I know how much you hate taking him out. But that's the kind of neighbor and friend you are, Lucas Rook. You're so caring." She turned away to exhale a stream of menthol smoke.

"Caring is sharing, Gracey. I'm going to leave now so I don't got to squat myself right here in your fancy living room."

"That's why I called, Lucas, I'm working on it so you don't have to."

"Usually I let those kinds of things just fly by, Gracey, but this I got to hear." Lucas unzipped his jacket and sat down. "Explain it to me that I don't have to shit on your rug."

She switched the cigarette to her other hand. "No, so you don't have to be a squatter, you don't have to squat. I mean, so you'll have a place to live."

"I appreciate your saying that, Grace Savoy. And I almost

understand you, which is making me nervous. Anyways, I think I'm good working out the financing."

Grace snubbed out her cigarette and walked towards him. "Hug," she said. "Just remember, I'll always be there if you need me. We help each other flourish, you know."

"Like those irises?"

"Sort of. And if you need some private financing, I'm only a point and a half over prime."

Rook went back to his apartment and worked the numbers again. No way he wasn't going to need something more than the credit union. In the meantime, Warden owed him two more checks on the Helen Maguire job. The retainer on the bone case was on its way, which meant time to get the billing going on that.

He called back over to the Brooklyn DA. Nobody called it "The Kings County DA," which is what it was, unless they were from Nebraska or whatever.

The detective running the case for Finklestein now was Mark Johnson, who used to be a big-time basketball player. They had worked on the Charlie Kolbik case together. Poor bastard was in love with the subway ever since he was a kid, rode all the routes for fun. Knew every stop on every line. Then after Nam he waits his turn in line until all the minorities got their jobs, and then he gets his. Gets it alright. First year on the job and he gets stabbed fifteen times from some pus bag just for the hell of it. Died right there on the A train.

Lucas did some more research on Sirlin's assignment. You meet with MJ O'Reilly, you have to know what you're doing. In another hour, he had enough to dazzle even her. They're having cocktails, he's titillating her with "ghouls," "harvests," and "body snatchers." Kevin McCarthy starred in the original *Invasion of the Body Snatchers*. Sam Peckinpah was an extra in the film. There were 400,000 bone grafts done in the last year, and cadaver bones and splinters were ground up for cement in orthopedic operations and dental filler. Another reason to dodge that next dentist appointment and the $1000 crown. Alistair Cooke's daughter is Susan Kitteredge. His stepdaughter Holly Rumbold. As tasty tidbits as those little hot dogs wrapped in blankets.

Rook also found an FDA web site that would yield good billing and the identity of two poor souls who reported receiving contaminated grafts, Patricia Battisti and Michael St. Denis. Battisti was local and suing Biomedical Tissue Services and Long Island Jewish Health Systems for allegedly passing along syphilis from improperly screened tissue. The FDA recall letter dated November 15, 2005, was also on the web and with a decent printer it would be a good addition to the file.

There also was Wendy Kogat, who learned that parts of her dead sister were removed. And of course, the sharks in the water. Massive amounts of lawsuits for "undue fear in patients" were not far behind. All that meant long-term, decent billing which Hugh Sirlin's black empire could well afford to pay.

You're meeting MJ O'Reilly you wear your Hollywood Detective outfit, black turtleneck, one of the jackets that Sarkissian was able to fit perfect enough to show off your shoulders and hide your gun.

Lucas stopped by Jimbo Turner's to get a touch-up on his black shoes and to check whether there had been any more vandalism.

"All quiet on the Western front," said the shineman. He leaned in close and ran his finger over the shoes. "These looking pretty good."

"Not too many fancy dates or funerals," Lucas said.

The shineman wiped on and off a coat of wash and then popped a new can of black polish. "Had my own funeral shoes on the other day. Tex died. Other than me and Joe Brinkley, who was the best shoe man there ever was, called him Joe Diamond, the way he made them shine. Other than Joe and me, he was the best."

Jimbo Turner wiped on some Vaseline and then took the

brushes clickety clack and did his rag, snapping and popping. He offered his shoulder for Lucas to get down. Rook paid him five and Jimbo brushed his jacket.

"Appreciate your looking after me," the shineman said.

Lucas nodded.

"All us good shinemen going to meet up in heaven someday," said Jimbo Turner.

Rook went on to his office. There was a message from Felix Gavilan, Esq. A self-promoting jerkwad, but somebody who sent business and paid his bills, two reasons to deserve a callback.

Gavilan got on sounding half like Ricardo Montalban doing a Corinthian leather commercial and half like a carnival barker. "You got my lovely calendar, Lucas?"

"Appreciate it, counselor. What can I do for you?"

"I'm calling about those grave robbing cases."

"You got something for me, Felix? I figured anybody would have one hand in Atlanta and one in New York, it would be you."

The lawyer got off the line and then got back on. "Actually, I was calling to invite you to find some work for both of us. There'll be hundreds of cases, all with defendants with deep pockets."

"Actually, Felix, I'm working the other side."

"That's not necessarily a bad thing. You find any bereft clients looking for a smooth lawyer with a killer instinct, you're author- ized, no, encouraged to sign them up. You don't have contingency fee agreements, I'll send them to you."

"I've got plenty, Felix," Rook lied. "And thanks for thinking of me."

"*De nada,*" said Gavilan.

"Ole," said Rook, and hung up.

The mail was late. Nothing in the fax machine, not even a bogus stock tip or reminder that he could buy any drugs he wanted without a medical exam.

The phone rang. Cholly Hepburn, psychologist to the stars. "I was returning your call," he said.

"Not me," said Lucas.

"Probably my answering service, they've been giving me make-up messages. And following me. Their disguises are quite convincing."

"Probably, Doc. What's up?"

The other line clicked in. It was Everett Warden. "Can I call you back, Cholly? I got to take this."

"You just did. I want you to take me to buy a gun."

"My pleasure, doctor."

"Pleasure? Let's talk about that. Give me a buzz. J. Edgar Hoover's been following me and he's wearing the same strapless number that I am."

Lucas switched over to the insurance man. "Just wanted to tell you to close your file," Warden said. "Things worked out just fine. In fact, you have another modest bill, get it right out to me."

Rook pulled the Maguire folder to see the last billing entries. "What happened, Dick?"

"We took a couple of righteous depositions after our 12B Motion and threatened them with Rule 11. So we settle the case. Marshall Funding gets to keep part of the proceeds assigned to them by Helen's son. We get to clear the claim and pay nothing on the Accidental Death."

"Very impressive," said Lucas Rook.

"Rule 11. Your lawsuit is bullshit. The court drops a ton on your head and you get assessed big time," said Warden. "Twelve B's the Motion to Dismiss we set it up with."

Lucas made a note to back-in billing for "Assess investigative material for possible settlement."

"You notify the brother yet that he's getting zilch?" Rook asked.

"Should have gotten the notice that he's not getting a dime."

"He won't be a happy camper."

"That could be a problem, Lucas, I understand, but your engagement by us on this matter is over. I sent a fax to that effect, but it didn't go through. Check your machine. It's important that you understand that you no longer represent the company in this matter. All of your actions are your own responsibility."

"Which is why you called me, Dick?"

"I also called to thank you for handling my situation."

"Appreciate that, Dick. You're a good guy." He is, he's the first in the insurance business.

Lucas checked his watch and his demanding, detailed schedule for the rest of the day. Send off some more billing on Maguire, get lunch, get pretty, allow MJ O'Reilly to tease or squeeze his balls, whatever made her feel more in charge. And now that he knew that the lump of human waste that was Reds Maguire was going to feel the world just put a hole in his head and fucked it, to leave some time to pay him a pre-emptive visit. Up the fire escape next door, across the flat roof, and then in through their flimsy-ass door. Break Eddie's other collarbone so he had a matched set and leave Reds Maguire with a permanent reminder not to fuck with him.

Rook was walking up to the deli when he got a bad vibe and saw the crowd. Any decent cop caught that kind of vibe even though he couldn't explain how. Lucas pushed his way through to the scene.

"You working this?" asked the newbie with the thin blonde moustache.

"Well, I must have 'NYPD' written all over me." Lucas looked at his nameplate. "Fine police work on that, Poppert. What you got for me?"

"Lady and her dog took a flyer off the roof. Like a big pile of pudding. Although the shepherd, a guide dog, like that, was still twitching and all. Maybe if it's a homicide the perp airmailed the pooch because he didn't want no witnesses."

The sergeant-in-charge walked over. "Another fine day in the neighborhood. You just can't get enough of it, Rook, or you just happening by?"

"Your patrolman Poppert there's a knucklehead, Sarge."

"Tell me something I don't know, Lucas. Meanwhile, you're looking like you're enjoying life nearly as much as me. And I'm so happy, I almost can't stand it."

"Sure, Sarge, sure," said Rook. No way would following the meat wagon in do him any good. Whatever he needed he could get soon enough without shining a spotlight on his head. The job was going to have plenty to say at the scene anyway, so he headed back to the St. Claire.

27

When Rook got back to the apartment house, the lobby was filled with detectives, street cops, a crew from Crime Scene on the way out, and the expected minorities from Community Relations.

One of the detectives, who should have known better, attempted to give Rook some shit.

"That's nice," Lucas told him. "I had my gold shield when you were still in elementary school."

"Still, I have to ask you some questions."

"No you don't," said Lucas.

"No he don't," said Detective Graves as he walked over. "I got this. Everything's cool."

"Old home week, Dwight," Lucas said.

"Nice building you got here, Rook. The bunch of real estate folks throwing up in the office over there about what this is going to do to the prices tell me it's going co-op or condo, whatever."

"That's what I hear, DG. Not going to be doing me any good."

"Been upstairs, of course. The bosses wanted us inside your place. I thought that showed disrespect, but you know how the job is nowadays."

Rook nodded.

They went upstairs. The elevator opened to another circus. Detective Graves waved them away. "You inviting me in, Rook? There's probably some beer left."

"Fuck me," said Lucas when he opened his door.

There was a uniform sitting on the sofa surfing through the cable.

"Take a hike, fuckface," Rook told him.

The cop looked up.

"After you empty your pockets."

"You're kidding? He's kidding about that, right, detective?"

"Probably about everything except your new nickname. Bye-bye, now."

Rook walked through his apartment. The place looked okay.

"Actually, we did find a pair of sweatpants under the sofa and the mystery of some of your missing socks has been solved," said Graves.

Rook sat down. "Let's get this over, Dwight."

"You got that cold beer?"

"Not going to happen. First, I don't like cops in my apartment, second I don't like thinking a friend of mine was a puddle on the sidewalk."

"And you don't like me," said Graves. "Going back to when Hy and I worked you a little bit over that perp got all fucked up in your buddy's garage."

"Or your little joke, Anthony D'Angelo is D'Angelo Anthony, the black man you're hinting at is Sicilian. Not to mention I got another beneficiary for my client who's a dead kid."

Dwight smoothed the sleeves of his sports coat. "Thought you had a sense of humor," he said.

Lucas went into the kitchen to get himself a can of Yuengling. He brought one for Dwight. "You don't get a glass."

Graves sat down on the armchair across from the sofa. "This is a dark motherfucker. Management should at least be replacing the bulbs up in the ceiling."

"I like it like this. Let's get this done. This is a one-beer conversation, DG."

"I was working the Helen Maguire case, Lucas. I'm working this. Word's out all over Hell's Kitchen, what's left of it, that you're responsible for the brother's not getting the insurance money."

"There was some insurance policy shit. Helen's kid..."

"Killed overseas, right?"

"Right," said Rook. "He sold out his interest in the insurance to one of them shyster funding outfits. I get the assignment, the lawyers get involved, doing what they do."

"And you tuned up Eddie Kelly for what?"

"He needed it."

"Probably true, Rook. And your neighbor friend you think's the DOA is going to be okay, Rook. Some doc, name's Meltzer, made a house call, and took her away to one of those fancy hospitals before all this drama. The realtor lady's ten floors down after babysitting the dog or whatever."

"Then we're done here," said Lucas. He finished his beer. "As soon as you tell me this is police business and to stay out of it."

Dwight put his empty on the end table. "It is and you probably won't. I'm running this case because I caught the original fall down job and this got to be her loser brother behind all that mess on the sidewalk." He got up. "I know you, Rook, and I knew your brother. So do us both a favor and let me handle this."

"Probably not," said Rook.

"I didn't think so. Then at least stay out of my way and don't give me something to come back at you for."

"I'll see what I can do, DG. I really will."

Lucas went through his place good. There were a couple of things missing. There always is. Two beers and the swimsuit issue of *Sports Illustrated*. Cops are always taking souvenirs and whatnot once they got the hang of what's important to a scene and what's not. No way there's not bras, panties and maybe all of Gracey's dope stash missing from next door.

He put his feet up and finished the last beer, wondering whether the price of his apartment would go up or down with the real estate lady doing her gymnastics off the roof. And it would make a difference if Grace moved out or not. Some ways, it would be like her to stay on general principle or whatever, but then again, somebody's there to kill you and your dog's not something you forget.

Best bet was it was Reds Maguire and his roomie sending a better message than splashing paint on a shoeshine stand. With the Westside boys still having some killing left in them, if he didn't take them out it would only be a matter of time before these two pukes or some shitbag needing a hundred bucks would be coming back again. Unless he didn't get to them first. That was going to happen with a certainty they would not forget.

With all the cops in the building there was no way the Bobbsey Twins were going to pay a visit for awhile. As likely as not though, they would try a hit at one of his likely places before going underground. Lucas called over to Joe Oren's place. Jeanie answered.

"Can I take your order?" she asked.

"It's 'may,' Miss NYU. Is your dad there?"

"He is, Uncle Lucas. And Daddy says that 'May I take your order?' is too pretentious and actually serves to impose an artificial barrier between us and our dining public."

"He does, does he?"

"Does what?" asked Oren.

"Joe. It's me. A couple of pieces of shit just tried to kill Gracey, or they thought it was her anyway. Some real estate lady and the guide dog got airmailed off my building."

"So you want me to keep an eye out."

"Jeanie anyway, Joe. Just until I get this taken care of."

"No problem. She's going on a ski trip in about an hour. Three or four days. In the meantime, you need me for anything?"

A call from Sid Rosen came in on the other line. "Everything okay, Lucas boy?"

"You heard about Gracey, Sid?"

"That colored cop was partnered with Hy Gromek called. The one who was out here when I got tuned up."

"He's just reminding me who he is, Sid, so I don't get his fancy clothes all ruffled. You tell him he looks like Bill Cosby, he loves that."

"I will next time, Lucas. Or maybe Rufus Thomas."

"Which is who, Sidney?"

"Teamed up with Robert 'Bones' Couch. One of those black tapdancing duos. Anyway, it's a terrible thing about your friend's dog. 'The better I get to know men, the more I find myself loving dogs.' Charles de Gaulle said that. You want me to get the Merc out?"

"I'll be by in about twenty minutes, Sidney. I want to take care of this before the rats get back into their holes."

Lucas reached Catherine at the intermission of the opera. Even though he soft-pedaled it as much as he could, she was pissed. "It never ends, does it," she said.

"I guess not," Rook told her. "Stay at your dad's."

As usual, Valerie was much less complex and invited Lucas over. He passed. There were things to do.

Rook went to Hell's Kitchen with bad intentions. His pair of .45's, a back-up, and a throw-down piece. When he drove down West 48th, there was a look-out at one end of the block and another pusbag leaning against the fence across the street from 444.

Rook started his turn at the corner, then jammed it into reverse. The far look-out beat feet, but Slips McClatchy wasn't so lucky. Lucas had him up against the corner of the fence and the barrel of his .45 pressed into his right eye.

"I don't, I don't..." said Slips.

"You don't what? You're doing something, aren't you?"

"I don't nothing."

"Too bad," said Lucas. "You were breathing. I thought that counted as something. Meanwhile, I'm about to pop your eye out. Then I'm going to blow a hole in you so you're going to spend your days crapping in a bag. Or…"

"Or what, or what?" said McClatchy.

"You tell your boyfriends Reds Maguire and Eddie Kelly that I'm coming for them."

Lucas lowered his Glock. "Go across the street and tell them if they're there." He took a roll of twenties out of his pocket. "And you can tell whoever the fuck that just booked around the corner. You give him a Jefferson, you take one. Go up to the newsstand, the corner tappy, even the Starbucks if you can stand it. You tell everybody everywhere you go that Lucas Rook is sitting over here against the fence waiting for them two sissies. Everybody you tell, you get twenty, they get twenty."

"That's fifty-fifty," said Slips. "Why should…"

"Don't fuck with me. I'll be here for two hours and back tomorrow same time for two more. You can make yourself some serious folding money, dirtbag. Just remember to tell everybody that I'm here and that them two are back-stabbing, dog killer faggots, and that Reds Maguire murdered his own sister for the blood money."

"You going to front me some of that currency?"

"Two more things," Lucas told him.

"Right."

"One, you try and fuck me, I'm going to pop your right eye out and then give you a new asshole. And two, I leave with Reds Maguire in the trunk of my car, there's an extra five hundred in it. An even grand for the two of them pusbags. Spread the word."

"You're serious," said Slips McClatchy.

Lucas peeled off some twenties. "As serious as a heart attack," said Rook. "Now you have a nice day."

28

Lucas Rook went around the corner and hit the newsstand for everything they had on the stolen bone cases. Lots of print now, but what would you expect with indictments coming down and the lawyers in a feeding frenzy. Not to mention the TV stations loving the funeral parlors with the secret operating rooms and the growing panic that somehow the dead could reach out from the grave and give you the syph or whatnot.

Lucas sat on the Clinton Gardens bench with a newspaper just below eye-level. About halfway through the *Times*, another one of the neighborhood's fine ambassadors walked up. "You looking for Reds and Eddie Kelly?"

"Going to take their picture for the society page here. What you got for me?"

The half a mope-junkie looked away and then back again. "I don't know nothing about no *picstures*. Only that you giving out twenties for their whereabouts." He offered a limp, dirty hand. The index finger was missing the last joint. "Name's Jack Queenan, John Joseph. People call me Queenie, though that's not my given name."

"Well, Jack. Thanks for the genealogy lesson or whatever. You got something for me?"

Queenan looked at him.

"Queenie, you got something for me, you got the twenty." He folded the newspaper and put it down. "You blow smoke, you take a beating."

"I'm speaking on both of them, I get two twenties?"

"Knock yourself. Now what do you got?"

Queenan rubbed his dirty hands together. "I got two things. One is Kelly. He's gone to Bayonne, which is where his sister is. He says until his arm heals up and then he's going to get you. And I heard him over at Boyle's speakeasy saying it was Reds' insurance money and he probably wasn't going to be seeing anything of it anyways. But he was coming for you personal and was going to cut you up while you was still breathing."

Lucas gave him a twenty.

"Other thing might be worth more, I'm thinking."

"And what's that?"

Queenan looked up the block and down. "I wouldn't be sitting here if I was you. Reds got himself a rifle, shotgun, something like that, paid a hundred for it and he means to blow a hole in you for sure."

Rook peeled off sixty dollars. "Nice doing business with you. Now you want to go tell either one of them mutts what you gave me, you just remember that beating I promised you."

Queenie rubbed his dirty hands together and went on up the block. Lucas looked at his watch. He wasn't wearing a vest and the rifle story could be as much bullshit as truth. But leaving early is saying you can be run off, which is just as likely to give some puke the guts to try and take you out for real when otherwise it was only barroom talk.

Rook went around the corner to the Brother's Deli at 49th and Ninth. Meatball sub and a Coke. Also a stop in the back for a Manhattan phone directory, which he stuffed in his windbreaker to finish his shift. Nothing happened.

He went over to his office with a little homework on Kelly, he was able to come up with a sister living in Bayonne. A quick run over there to show he meant business and knew about Reds' rifle would be a good thing.

The phone rang. It was Gracey. "I'm okay, neighbor," she said. "Okay for a blind girl, they killed her best friend after they meant to kill her. Dr. Meltzer said Argos was probably dead before he…" She started to cry, then stopped. "Can you bring me cigarettes? They told me I can smoke, but I can't have them."

Rook took his Kevlar vest from the closet. "Where are you, Gracey?"

"Silverhill, Goldenhill. Blueberry Hill. One of those. Are you coming now?"

"I'll be out soon. Meanwhile, you're in good hands, Gracey."

"Sure I am. First they kill all the flowers, then my dog. They're after me, Lucas Rook. I'm as blind as a bat and I can see that."

"Who's they, Grace?"

"Well, those real estate moguls, that's who. They want to break us apart. Sure, my eyes are dead, dead as those irises in New Jersey, but they know I can see things, see what they're thinking, what they're planning."

"And what's that, Grace Savoy?"

"I'll tell you when I see you, neighbor. I'll tell you true."

You're blind and somebody tries to whack you, throws your guide dog and realtor friend off the roof, no way you're not acting batshit. And only a little bit better when you find out it's some washed-up Westside gangsters, thinking it's payback for something had nothing to do with you.

Lucas got the Merc to run over to Bayonne and pay Eddie a call. The Holland Tunnel to Exit 14A to Bayonne should have taken twenty-five minutes. Best thing of the place was Chuck Wepner, the Bayonne Bleeder. Got over a hundred stitches losing to Sonny Liston, knocked Ali down, which inspired *Rocky* for which he got bupkas. Night of the fight, Wepner buys his wife a fancy nightgown, tells her tonight she's sleeping with the champ of the world. After Chuck loses, she says, "Ali coming to my room or I'm going to his?"

Lucas followed Avenue D, you didn't know better you called the street between C and E "Broadway." Megan Fogg lived on 27th Street. She weighed 300 pounds if she weighed an ounce and hadn't seen her brother Eddie in six years, since he was sent away to Rahway for keeps, poor dear. So much for that twenty bucks.

Rook stopped for a piece of pie and two cups of coffee at a place called Robert's. There were brochures at the register for two-bedroom townhouses, "starting at just $595,000." So much for Jersey.

Lucas drove by the Maguire-Kelly homestead when he got back to Manhattan, just to let everybody know he was around. As he was heading downtown, he saw Queenan come out of the Dunkin Donuts.

"I'll be by tomorrow for my refund, you lying cocksucker," Rook said. "Be where I can find you."

You had a neighborhood, or a "constituency," as Tuzio used to call it when he knew his ass from his oatmeal, you had somebody to go to. The snitch, the post office, the king of the neighborhood. Lucas needed to get the skinny on what was going on in Hell's Kitchen, he went to Cronin.

No nickname or anything like that, not even a first name, but Cronin either directed everything that went on in the part of the Kitchen that hadn't gotten all gentried-up, or was in on it one way or another.

The office door in the back of the floor-covering shop was always unlocked, but you always knocked, lest you open the door and find yourself splattered by a tripped 12-gauge.

The store was all boxes of black and white tile, self-stick. Drums of adhesive. Rolls and rolls of outdoor-indoor carpet, perfect if you wanted your home to be a miniature golf course. Cronin was in his office, flipping through the stacks of manufacturer's coupons that his army of deserted housewives and heavy drinkers had clipped out of the magazines and newspapers for him.

"You check for your Ed McMahon's sweepstakes or whatever?" Lucas asked.

"You looking hard for Reds and Eddie Kelly, you're papering the neighborhood with twenties the way you are?"

Rook laid down five twenties.

"Buy a lot of weekly periodicals with that," said Cronin. "I appreciate it, the respect. Well, I have not seen their sorry asses, which I suppose is their good fortune, Reds and Eddie Kelly. I do see them or hear they're moving about I will call you."

"Appreciate that," said Lucas.

"Which is my permission for you to do to them whatever."

"Appreciate that, too," Rook said. And he went on to see Jockey Joe. Bad joke it was to call him that. Short enough to be a jockey he was, 4 foot 11 in his stocking and now almost that big around. Jockey Joe was at his laundromat making change. He had little to say other than how hard it was to make a living anymore.

A couple of more stops to get a line on the Westsider pukes. A trip by the Stroll to ask around, though it was unlikely that either Reds or Eddie Kelly would be shelling out their cash for streetwalkers when there were always the toothless neighbor ladies.

Kittie Knowlton was running her enterprise from the black Continental with the suicide doors. "Miss Amy did it like she said she would, leaving me behind to manage things."

"And how's that, Kittie K?" Rook said.

"I occupy myself with the business end. Keep the books, see the girls get their check-ups and whatnot. Just remember what Ms. Amy told me, keep Shavon and Big Leonard from beating up on folks, and folks from beating on Crystal Lee. You looking for Crystal Lee? She always thought kindly of you."

"Looking for two Hell's Kitchen old timers, Reds Maguire,

Eddie Kelly."

Leon walked over, wriggling like he wasn't 6'2", 210 lbs. "I need to lay down, Ms. Kittie."

"That's what we do, dearie. Now you go on."

"I'm dizzy, Ms. Kittie," said Leon.

"Then put your head down," Kittie said.

Leonard walked away adjusting his big thong.

"That's kind of a joke I made, Mr. Rook. I'm starting to see things different now that I'm management. I ain't seen those two fellows you described. Meanwhile, I got to get back to my office."

She opened the big doors of the Lincoln. "You're welcome to an appointment any time. Like Ms. Amy said, always remember the clientele."

Lucas gave her his business card. "Feeling's mutual. Call me if you need something."

Rook swung by Shirl Frelang's newsstand at Broadway and 23rd. She had the ear of the streets and owed him big time for directing her to Warren G. Phelps, Esquire, to help her with the cigarette tax thing. Warren charged like an Iraq defense contractor, but with results so you didn't mind.

Shirl was not there. There was an Arab making change.

"She here?" Lucas asked.

"I'm the new proprietor, sir. And I am from Spain. Ms. Frelang has retired to be in Florida with her father, sir."

Lucas walked away. Shirl was good people. So was Amy. "I'd double-bag the Pope" was a worthy legacy. Maybe Amy and Shirl would run into each other at the dog track or at Disney.

Rook's cell phone rang.

"You owe me that steak and seven-fifty," said Dwight Graves.

"The steak I remember you trying to get on the arm. Explain me the seven-fifty, detective."

"Word on the street was you were paying twice that to get those two ass-wipes in the trunk of your vehicle. Well, yours truly and those fine members of the NYPD who are still compelled to work this rotten job got them in lockdown. The Tombs, no visitors, no bail. Giving you two-fifty off, law enforcement discount."

"Another one for New York's finest. Appreciate the call, Dwight."

29

Joe Oren was just sitting himself down at the counter when Rook came in to tell him the coast was clear.

"Take a load off, Lucas. Have some coffee and some pie," said Joe. "Only you may have to help me back up again."

"No problem, pardner. Back out again?"

"Out and around the block." He popped a Flexeril. "Hate these damn things. Only thing that helps, but they make me goofy. That and the ice packs. The frozen peas, I mean."

"Which means I skip that on the menu," said Lucas.

Sam came out from the back. "That and the apple pie, unless you don't care what's going into your bloodstream, because I did not bake them, so I can't tell you where the fruit's coming from." He poured three cups of coffee.

"Done," said Rook. "That and that other thing I called about. The murdering pricks are in the system."

"Saves them from being dead," said Oren.

"Or worse," said the cook.

Jeanie came in the front door. She had her backpack over her right shoulder and her left arm behind her back.

"You bring your dear old dad some posies or some maple

syrup or something from your ski trip?"

"Something like that, Daddy." She brought her arm around in a purple cast up to her elbow.

Joe got himself off the stool. "You alright, Jeanie? What happened?"

"It's okay. They call it a buckle fracture which I googled on somebody's laptop on the bus on the way back, which means like a greenstick or something." She put her backpack down and fished for the hospital papers.

Sam brought her a cup of tea and some aspirins. "You sit down, Jeanie."

"Almost hit the doctor though. I know when something's broken." She looked at the discharge page. "More interested in how her hair looked than anything. She kept calling me dear. I said you better give me an x-ray because I knew better."

"Aren't you supposed to keep it up?" Lucas said.

"I did the whole way back."

"They give you anything for the pain, Jeanie? I'll get you in to see Doc Lawinski, who I'm seeing for my back tomorrow."

"They gave me some Motrin. One of the kids had some Percs. So I took them."

"How many did you take?" asked Rook.

Sam brought the pie out and Jeanie stuck her finger in everybody's meringue.

"Six or so. Maybe four. I forget."

"No you didn't," said Joe.

"No, I didn't, Daddy. I'm only halfway stupid. I'm sorry about your back."

"Nothing stupid about you, Jeanie. It's skiing that's stupid."

"Only if you think sliding down the mountain on some little sticks ain't smart," said Sam.

"Over ice-covered, jagged rocks," said Joe. "Let's both go recuperate. Lawinski will see us tomorrow morning."

"I got class, Daddy."

"So you'll miss one."

"You twisted my arm," she said. And she started to laugh. "Must be the Percocets."

"Hand them over," said Joe. "They're very addictive."

"So's Sam's pie, Daddy. Besides, I don't have any more."

"I got Tylenol 3's if you want them," said Rook. "Got a meeting tonight so I'll drop them off if you want."

"Is your meeting pretty?" said Jeanie.

"Not as pretty as you," said Lucas. "Now keep that arm elevated. Anybody needs me, use my cell."

Rook drove over to Sid Rosen's to return the Merc. The garageman was just coming around the corner with his dog.

"How's it going, Lucas boy?"

"Seems that chapter's about over with. Which reminds me, I'll get you your book back tomorrow. I've only got two chapters to go. Going up to the Muskrat's. You want anything, Sid?"

"Who knows what he has? Canned peaches. Bird flu masks, work socks. He got some decent insulated underwear and dog food, no beef."

"Cash and carry, Sidney."

"Alright. But you see anything for Bear, here, you can carry, just go ahead. I'll take care of it."

"We'll call it even on the late fines for the book."

"Which is called?" asked Sid.

"Something by Robert Conrad."

"Joseph Conrad, Lucas boy. Robert's the one who played Pappy Boyington."

"Right, right. Did those battery commercials. I could never tell them apart."

Lucas called Catherine Wren, but had to leave a message. "Everything's okay. If you're staying at your dad's, maybe I could run you home."

Rook walked over to Muskrat's, but had to flex his bad leg before he started the four flights up.

"Well, look who it is, still New York's finest, what can I do you for?" asked Muskrat.

"Got to give somebody some cigars."

"You wanting it to look like it costs how much?"

"Nothing crazy. Maybe fifty," Lucas told him.

"Raymundo, bring me the Nate Shermans, just came in. Retail for fifty-five, cost you twenty-five, Rook. You take two, you're still ahead."

The Mexican came over with a half dozen boxes of the Skyline Collection. Lucas put one on the counter.

"You like this sweater I'm wearing, Rook? Pure cashmere. For you, seventy bucks."

"Not my style, Muskrat."

"I'm a mohair man myself, Rook. You know. I got mo' hair than anybody's not in the zoo. Except on my head, of course."

"Just adds to your charm. You got any dog treats or whatever?"

"Raymundo, get me one of those bags of rawhide thingies," the wholesaler said. "Shaped like dicks they are. Anything else?"

"You got black work socks?"

"I do," said Muskrat. "But you know the latest studies show that nylon socks are the best to prevent blisters."

"Can't do nylon," said Rook. "Makes me feel like a lawyer or a pimp. Same difference I guess."

"A dozen of the 316's," the wholesaler called as he came out from behind the counter. He was wearing a pair of shoes that looked like they were from the '70s. "You like these kicks?" he said. "Can you believe I paid six bucks a pair? Six bucks. For six bucks I'm not going to pass them up. You want a couple of pairs? Sell them to you for ten."

"I'm good to go," Lucas said.

"You only think you are, Rook. Follow me." He walked Lucas across the floor and opened a padlocked door. "These just came in. Got them at a Customs seizure sale. You say 'no' to these, I'm going to cry."

The little room was filled with piles of leather coats. "What are you, 46-48?"

"48-50. Depends."

"Depends if you're packing. Which, by the way, you can always talk to me about if you're looking to purchase or sell."

"No, I can't."

"No you can't. Try this." He picked out a leather trenchcoat. "It's like butter."

"Not for me."

"Right, right," said Muskrat.

He went to a different pile and pulled out a black leather sports coat. "Now that's what I'm talking about. Cole Haan. Lists for $795."

"Eight hundred bucks, that's a car, not a jacket."

"Right, right. Try it on. Fit you like a glove."

Lucas tried on the jacket. Perfect for his meeting with MJ O'Reilly. "How much?"

"Half. No, three bills."

"I'll give you two and a quarter."

Muskrat started to put it back. Then handed it over. "You're killing me, Rook. I mean you're not right." He did his little Muskrat laugh. "Ray, come bag this up."

Rook handed over his plastic.

"I usually charge an extra 15% you're charging, but it's my pleasure."

"You're a prince, Muskrat. You surely are," Lucas said. "And I love your shoes."

Rook went back to his apartment at the St. Claire.

Jim Dunlop was sitting in the lobby. Rook went over. "How you doing, detective," he said.

"Moonlighting. How's retirement?"

"Keeping busy. You?"

"Building supers have me here for show since that flyer job," Dunlop said. "I got my eye on your place, though. Shame about that lady, though. Friend of yours?"

"Nope, Jimmy. You need to take a piss or have a cold one or whatever, stop on by."

"Already did," Dunlop said. "Just kidding. Tape's still up next door. You get any overflow work, give me a holler."

"Will do," Rook said. "Will do."

Lucas went up to his apartment. Three calls from Gracey. At least she was feeling better enough to be her crazy self. He called her back, but she was sleeping, probably sedated so she wasn't annoying the other guests. And a message from Catherine that she wouldn't want to disappoint her father and maybe the three of them could meet for brunch at which could he not wear a gun that would show.

He checked his messages at the office. Another call from Felix Gavilan, Esq. "Call me if you have anything." And a call from Mark Johnson at the Brooklyn DA which he did return. "Appreciate your call, Mark."

"No prob. Finks said to give you what I got. You're working some of this boneyard mess?"

"If I'm lucky," Lucas said.

"This is going to be like one of them big Hollywood porno films. Civil suits coming up all over the place. You know the word is a corpse is worth a hundred grand. Anyways, Rook, we're doing some exhumations and looking at a bunch of funeral parlors here in Manhattan. We got a couple of cases up where the bodies disappeared between the church and the crematorium and wound up in a chop shop we're just waiting to take down. I'll let you know. Meanwhile, I got to run."

"Take it light," said Rook.

"Any way I can get it," said Johnson.

Lucas ran a hot tub for his bad leg and the old wounds from

where Etillio and his punk-ass strong arms beat him bad in their garage. They should have killed him there rather than torture him. It would have saved them a lot of dying.

Afterwards, Rook poured a cold one and got some more billing off the web. Two lawsuits had been filed in Atlantic County, New Jersey: *Augustin v. Medtronic* and *Pieper v. Medtronic Funeral Homes*. He cross-referenced all funeral homes mentioned in the probes and SDA's holdings, but found no hits. His search did turn up a book written by Mastromarino, the dental surgeon everybody was calling the mastermind behind the body harvesting. The book was called *SMILE*. I wonder if he's smiling now.

As Lucas was shaving, he went over the last job he did for SDA and how he was going to work Ms. MJ O'Reilly. "Seamless transition" was what the giant funeral corporation was all about, whether it was dealing with the state attorney general's investigation of their funeral homes deals with the synagogues or the jobs he was working on for them.

He had worked the "hearse ghoul" job for SDA, somebody boosting their hearses and whacking off on their corpses. The first part was easy, grabbing up the ex-con who was fencing the vehicles through some Long Island "dead sled" dealer. The second part was more complicated, SDA catching their own employee "red-handed" using their sophisticated internal surveillance. Not kosher to have one of your own beating his meat on the dearly departed. Not a good thing either that you're running tape on everything going on in your funeral homes. First, you got the privacy issues can get you sued. And you're making a record of shit maybe you don't want to remember.

MJ O'Reilly was the typical New York corporate cunt. Business suits with expensive shoes that had just the right amount of fuck me fashion. She smoked heavy, drank well and lived in an SDA-owned apartment. MJ had no television, stereo, books or paintings.

Lucas looked through his closet. Not much there, but with the new leather sportscoat, he was able to put together a look that even she would approve of.

Rook was in the lobby of the St. Claire giving Dunlop a chance to drain his vein when MJ got him on the phone. For once her formal affect was gone.

"Our dinner meeting is cancelled," she said. "In fact, so am I, frankly, for reasons I do not understand. Maybe they think I know too much about how they do business. Hugh Sirlin, the shriveled prick, even told me that I should vacate my apartment, actually their apartment, as they say it."

"Sorry to hear that, MJ. Is there anything I can do?"

She lit a cigarette. "If they don't cancel you out too, Mr. Rook, you can do a number of things. One, you can tell Mr. Sirlin, if you speak to him, that he hasn't heard the last of me. Two, you can stand by because my lawyer will want to talk to you. And three, if you're looking as good as you did last time, you can meet me at the Pink Elephant."

"What time you thinking about, MJ? I've got another meeting."

"Sure, sure. You're probably in on it too. But no matter, I'm into my third or fourth Cosmo, so frankly, you can go fuck yourself if you so desire."

"I'll see you soon, Ms. O'Reilly. In the meantime, take it easy. Everything will work out."

He took a cab over to the Pink Elephant. At the very least, he'd get a billable meeting out of it and if his assignment with SDA was in jeopardy, maybe come up with enough information to protect it. Rook was out of the taxi and crossing at 27th St. when a dark panel truck ran the light. He had to dodge quickly as the truck swerved and then sped away.

30

Miata's was a good cop bar, which was getting harder and harder to find. There were unmarkeds parked all over the place and a couple of blue and whites since there was no lot. John Morris and Ferris, who had been partnered up since as long as he could re-member, were coming down the block and behind them a bad oiler, who likely was using the spot as a pitstop so he could convince him-self that he wasn't all the way in the bottle.

Dobie was behind the bar wearing his ever-present derby. "Good evening, detective," he said.

Safe bet even though he'd only been in a couple of times. "Dwight here yet, Obie?"

"I'm Dobie. Obie's my brother."

"You sure about that? He just told me the same thing."

"Good one," said Andi, who almost knocked somebody out when he was in before.

Dobie tipped his hat and drew them each a draft. Freddie Galen came over, working at the place now instead of being a scrounging pain in the ass since he got religion.

"Table, booth or counter?" he asked.

Lucas saw Graves sitting in the back. "I got reservations," he said.

Dwight was sipping on a Crown Royal with an empty glass next to it.

"You keeping count?" Rook asked him.

"Don't want nobody padding my tab. Then I can't be wearing a seven, eight-hundred-dollar jacket."

Lucas sat down. "Hoping to find you here."

"Hoping to show your appreciation that our finest grabbed up those Westsider leftovers."

Freddie Galen came over with two menus. "Shrimp, chicken in the basket. Beef and roast pork is good."

"I don't eat swine and don't want it at my table neither, Freddie G-whizz. Now, bring me another, and brother Lucas here's going to want a beer."

Detective Graves finished his drink. "Man needs a *see-gar* when he's drinking Crown Royal. You hear me saying *see-gar* instead of *cigar* means I'm comfortable with myself."

The waiter came over with their drinks. "You ordering?"

"Ordering you not to be ruining my appetite," Dwight told him.

Lucas drank his beer, then handed over the cigars.

Graves opened the packet and sampled their aroma. "Lovely little sampler," he said.

"Appreciate your keeping me in the loop, DG. Even after you had me doing circus tricks," said Rook.

"Hy told me you were a surly prick. Not that I couldn't tell with my fine detective skills."

Lucas Rook lifted his glass. "To your partner," said Lucas. "*Fidelis ad mortem*." The police motto, "Faithful until death." Graves had said that the last time they sat together.

"What that jacket set you back, Lucas Rook? Cost you at least seven-fifty."

"Less than half."

"You're shitting me."

"I do not lie," said Rook.

Graves smoothed his cashmere jacket. "Tell you what, you call your haberdasher, he fit me up with a 42 long, we're even on the seven fifty."

"Thought you had your mind set on a thick steak, Dwight."

"Can't keep my lady waiting, detective."

"I hear that," said Lucas.

Detective Graves left and Rook called over the waiter. "Roast pork, mustard and raw onions," Rook told him. "And another Michelob."

The cab driver was a smart ass. "The St. Claire," he said. "They'll be calling it *St. Elsewhere* from what I hear."

Rook checked the guy's name tag for later.

"That was some old TV show, right?" said Lucas.

"That it was. *St. Elsewhere*. People will be moving 'elsewhere' and the apartment house will be like a show in reruns."

"Make believe, wasn't it?" said Rook. "Just like the tip you're not getting."

Jim Dunlop wasn't stationed in the lobby or anybody else, unless they were doing a magnificent job of disguising themselves as furniture or as Ribai, the night man, who gave a big, white smile.

Lucas went upstairs. Somebody new got on as the elevator door was about to close. Typical New York lawyer type. "Hurry up, honey," he told his horsey wife who was trying to make it across the lobby in heels that no way could support her 180-plus.

"Sorry," said the lawyer. He tried small talk about the building, but Rook gave him nothing back.

The wife adjusted the velvet bow behind her head, one of the world's greatest pastimes, pretending you came over on the May-flower. The lawyer and his wife were surprised that Rook was riding to a higher floor.

"Did you see that jacket?" she said as they were getting off. "He looked like a real gangster."

"Quiet," her husband said. "Mafia."

The crime tape was still up on Gracey's apartment. Too long, especially if she'd be home soon. He went into his dark apartment, just the one bulb in the standing lamp and the bathroom door partially open. But he knew where everything was, from his Smith and Wesson .45 to the picture of Kirk and him on the mantelpiece.

Usually he clicked on the TV, but the last cold one of the day might have to wait for tomorrow. Lucas hung up his new leather jacket. Maybe he'd get a padded hanger or whatever, but probably not.

Rook celebrated ending another day in The Naked City with a good piss. Then he hit the rack. The dreams were waiting like a bad relative. Him, Dwight Graves and Kirk wearing derbies like Dobie or Obie, whichever, had on. Hy Gromek or Tuze was saying something, but he couldn't make it out.

The phone rang, which first he thought was in the dream, but then he got it. It was Grace Savoy.

"Didn't wake you, did I, honey?"

"Never, Grace, whenever you call me in the middle of the night. You alright?"

"See you soon, honey."

"You're feeling better, Gracey. They discharging you?"

"Sort of. I threatened the shit out of them. You know, Section 1983 of the Civil Rights Act. Quoted them *Beltz v. New York*. You've been IOC more than once, you know the ropes."

"The Olympics, Gracey? I'm going back to sleep. Do what the doctors say. Get better."

"Not the International Olympic Committee, honey. IOC, Involuntary Outpatient Commitment. Been through that a dozen times. My parents thought a residential facility was a waste of money, when you subtract what you're paying for room and board is what IOC is, they used to say. But what are you going to do, honey, when both your parents are accountants and you're blind as a bat and like that."

"Grace. You stay there. I'll come up and see you. Now go to sleep."

"Nightie, nightie," she said. "See you soon, honey."

Crazy shit in the real world was easier to deal with than the fucked-up cartoons in his head. Lucas fell back to sleep anyway.

In the morning, he made himself a couple of scrambled eggs and a cup of bad coffee and went up to 166 to put together some kind of report to take over to Hugh Sirlin at SDA. The gang was out front of his office building on Fifth Avenue. Rook rolled his paper bag closed tight so his coffee didn't taste like Marlboro from walking through the haze. Some of the old faces were gone from when the rent went up, but there were new smokers there to replace them.

The designer guy who had made his business cards followed Rook into the lobby.

"They working for you, 'check-mate' and whatever?" he said.

"Absolutely," Lucas said.

"You need anything for promotion, we do that too." He took a drag from the cigarette he was palming. "You stop by, I got a whole catalogue and whatnot."

"Absolutely," Lucas told him. He hated salesmen almost as much as lawyers, who were salesmen charging you for them arguing that up was down, right was wrong. Except for Phelps, who's proving it's true.

The answering machine was flashing. Reminder 1000 to come in and get his teeth cleaned. Rook sat down and enjoyed the decent cup of coffee before he started on the report for Sirlin. He had plenty of research on the body-snatching, including ten possibles in Philadelphia, the corporations, Mastromarino. The preliminary info from the Brooklyn DA was good. He thought about taking out how MJ was going all cunty, but left it in because maybe it was some loyalty test or whatever.

When the report was done, Lucas went into Timeslips to generate a bill just in case she was giving him the straight skinny that his assignment was in jeopardy. He was moving stuff around on the screen to make sure he had the numbers he needed when the mailman or whoever was at the door.

"Package delivery. I can leave it."

Probably some promotional crap from Felix Gavilan, Esq. A different carrier, two, three times a week, but always the jingling of the keys coming down the hall. And the UPS, they required a signature.

Somebody wanted him to receive their little present up close and personal. Rook was just under his desk when the pipe bomb blew his door off. The new sprinklers were soaking his office and the alarms in the hall were ringing.

Rook got up. The concussion had him woozy and his ears were fucked. The explosion cut his room to ribbons with roofing nails. The kind of shit the mob used to do, like taking out Chicken Man Testa. An oldie but goodie, which could include the Italians or the Irish. Or somebody wanting it to look like that.

The question was answered by what was left of Eddie Kelly. Always do what you do best, and apparently bomb-making wasn't the hump's strong suit. Rook went down the back stairs before the fire engines and the PD showed up.

Reds Maguire was going to be celebrating somewhere and on his way to getting dead. Lucas eyeballed across the street and went a couple of blocks in each direction. Two bars and a restaurant got a good look, but the prick wasn't there.

Next stop was the Hell's Kitchen places. Get in and out and get to the next one before the word spread. The pus bag wasn't at Mike's or McCoy's or Jewey's old place, which had just changed its name again. Even a couple of the fancy spots, "pet friendly" and which hadn't had a camphor cake in the urinal in about thirty years.

Next best bet was Reds' apartment unless he was getting out of Dodge or doubling back. Maguire's place was empty. Underwear in the drawers. Two cartons of cigarettes and an old .38 revolver. No way he leaves that stuff behind.

Lucas did some doors and came up with nothing. The prick could be anywhere and the world was a big place to hide, so it made more sense to go back to the St. Claire, but with your smeller working overtime. Just because Reds Maguire was a piece of human garbage didn't mean he wasn't cunning. Hide out and finish the job and get some insulation from what happened at 166 Fifth Avenue at the same time. "Gee whiz, what would I be doing here if I had tried to blow him up somewheres else?"

The lobby had calmed down. Detective Dunlop with his paper. The tenants coming and going. Rook got on the elevator with the rich lady, who did her Martha Ray schtick. "Fifth floor, sporting goods," she said. "I've got to check their balls." Then she held the door and turned. "I hope you'll be staying on with us. You're such a dear."

Right, if somebody doesn't beat me to it and I'm dead or I don't have the sheckels to buy my apartment or the new management has other ideas.

He went the final two floors by the fire stairs. The crime scene tape was still up at Grace's.

His apartment dark as it always was, the one standing light on and the bathroom door open so the mirror on it gave him a good look around. But something wasn't right. You could always see the mantelpiece where he usually put his .45 when he came in next to the picture of him and Kirk getting their gold shields.

Rook rushed up his short entry hall into the front closet for cover and to check on the .357 he kept there for backup. The revolver wasn't there. In one swift move he ducked out and fired four quick shots into the bathroom. A lot of noise and property damage that his escrow wouldn't cover, but no Reds Maguire.

Lucas grabbed his other Glock from the bedroom and went out across the patio to Grace Savoy's apartment and pulled the yellow tape. All the doors were locked. He went back across to air his place out and wait for Dunlop to come upstairs if somebody was going to complain about his cannon going off or for whoever had his .357 to take their shot.

Rook was cleaning up the shards of bathroom tile when he heard the footsteps in the hall. You're a regular person you don't hear such things, you're a cop who's always at it, you always do.

Good news travels fast. Bad news faster. Reds Maguire was coming in the open door with the barrel of his sawed-off shotgun leading the way. This time the heavy rounds of Lucas Rook's Glock hit more than bathroom wall. Maguire jumped like the scene in *Bonnie and Clyde* as Lucas hit him with a half-dozen rounds from his .45.

"You mother fucker, coming here." Rook stood over him. "Now you can say hello to Eddie boy." He put a round between his eyes for good luck.

Lucas was finishing a beer when Dwight Graves showed up.

"Busy, busy day," he said. "You got one of those cold ones for me?"

Rook got him one and a second for himself. They went out on the patio where they could breathe some air that didn't have lead in it.

"Like I said, Detective Rook, busy day. You got something you want to tell me?" Dwight said.

"I was going to ask you the same thing, DG."

"Meaning what?"

"Meaning you told me those two dead perps were in the system."

"Not right you blaming me for Department of Corrections bullshit, Rook. That's not right. Maybe for my little jokes about Helen's boyfriend and their baby and all." He took one of the gift cigars out of his jacket pocket and lit up, turning it slowly to catch the flame. "One of the fine collection you gave me, Rook." He turned his head to blow the smoke away and shot Lucas twice.

Rook and the chair went over.

"*Fidelis ad mortem*," said Graves. "'Faithful until Death,' the Department's motto. You should have left it at that. But all you did was fuck things up after your brother got it."

He moved Rook's guns out of reach.

"Your twin brother you're going all avenging angel for, he got what he had coming, being the dirty cop he was."

Lucas Rook's breath was gurgling blood in his lungs, but his eyes widened.

"Etillio took him in on my recommendation," Graves went on. "And then took him out because not only was Kirk a dirty cop, he was running a game on the people who were paying him."

He took another puff of his cigar. "Made me look bad. You know how hard it is for a man of color, no matter how well he dresses, to get hired by the Italians. So everything's straightened out when Kirk's done, but then you go and do Etillio and his crew and my paydays are out the window.

"Now I've cleaned things up here, Lucas Rook, like you cleaned up those Hell's Kitchen boys. I appreciate that. Reds and Eddie knew Kirk was bad, which could wash up on me. No sense having them around to jeopardize my pension, now is there?" Dwight flicked his ash. "The four of you can sit around in Hell and play gin rummy or whatever. Meanwhile, I'll be saying goodbye to you, Lucas Rook. '*Fidelis ad mortem*.'"

There was the unmistakable sound of a hammer being cocked. Detective Graves turned to see Grace Savoy with a silver .357 in her hand.

"I'm a police detective, miss," he said. "And you're naked as a jaybird." Graves put his hand on his service weapon. "And from the look of things, you're blind. So why don't you just put that heavy pistol down? Everything's under control."

"You shot my friend. I'm not deaf," she said. "And you killed my dog. You tried to kill me, but I wasn't there and you threw my dog off the roof." Gracey started to cry.

Graves moved to pick up one of Rook's .45's. "We got the

men who did that, dear. Nobody's here to hurt you." He had the weapon and the angle he wanted.

Grace Savoy lowered the big gun, and then raised it up again, firing as she did. The hollow points tore through Graves' stomach, chest and neck. "You moved, you knelt, you got back up. I'm blind, mister, but like I told my neighbor, Lucas Rook, I can hear a pigeon fart a mile away."

She found Lucas lying on the patio. He was still alive, hearing the sirens he'd heard a thousand years ago when he came rushing down to save his twin brother, Kirk, who was bleeding out.

"I called for help before I shot that devil dead," said Grace Savoy.

She sat down and held Rook's hand.

"You'll be fine now, Lucas Rook. You have a whole life to lead and lots of things to do. We can plant flowers here on our patio. Irises, I think." She lit a cigarette. "The World's just filled with ugly, isn't it?"

Mark your calendar for the next release in the award-winning *Lucas Rook Mystery* series.

Coming Fall 2007

Blood Redeemed